Playground Wizard

By

RON OSTLUND

PublishAmerica
Baltimore

© 2013 by Ron Ostlund.
All rights reserved. No part of this book may be reproduced, stored in a retrieval system or transmitted in any form or by any means without the prior written permission of the publishers, except by a reviewer who may quote brief passages in a review to be printed in a newspaper, magazine or journal.

First printing

All characters in this book are fictitious, and any resemblance to real persons, living or dead, is coincidental.

PublishAmerica has allowed this work to remain exactly as the author intended, verbatim, without editorial input.

Softcover 9781630000189
PUBLISHED BY PUBLISHAMERICA, LLLP
www.publishamerica.com
Baltimore

Printed in the United States of America

Dedication

When I attended grade school you could go home for lunch if you lived close enough. We were two blocks away and, following the tradition established by my older brothers, I ate at home. When I arrived a toasted cheese sandwich and a bowl of tomato soup were waiting. The radio soap opera *Our Gal Sunday,* the story that asked if an orphan girl from a mining town in the west can find happiness as the wife of a wealthy and titled Englishman, had started. It was fifteen minutes long and before the next one, *The Romance of Helen Trent,* was over I was on my way back to school, but not the way I'd come home. I cut across our backyard, hurried down an alley only locals knew was there, dashed across Main Street where no crossing guards were posted, slipped between two apartment buildings, jumped on a small retaining wall, and climbed over a chain link fence. When I touched down on the other side I was standing on the school playground, a place of continual wonder to me. It was where boys became men and when the bell rang calling them to class, turned back to boys again. We played kickball in fair weather or foul and the game after lunch was the hardest fought.

This book is dedicated to the boys in the 1948, 7th grade at Rollins Elementary School for whom attending class was what you did between kickball games.

Contents

Wish Wizards Inc. 7
Stupid Nameover 25
Ear Island 36
Fine Print 45
BeWilbered 58
Kick It Here 69
Away Game: *Part 1: The Eindorf Connection* 82
Away Game: *Part 2: The Meaning of Air* 93
Top Banana 106
AfterMath 120
Third Grade Dance 136
The Day The Earth Stood Still 146
Rong Address 158
Curly Fleeman, New And Used Words 174
The Visit 194
Playground Wizard 206

Chapter 1
WISH WIZARDS INC.

J. Brandon Yarlboro, newest member of the sales force at *Twain's Twine,* stood at the entrance to *Doorman Brothers Awning and Supply.* He was wearing the standard Twain uniform; white shirt, red tie, gray slacks, and black shoes. On the pavement next to his feet was his sample case with *Twain's Twine* stenciled on both sides. Below the company name, in smaller print, was their motto; *"If it's not Twain, it's not twine."*

A braided string holding his employee identification card with, "Hi! I'm Yarl," printed below his picture, looped around his neck.

It looked like someone tried to remove *Brothers* from the sign on the front window of the store and either lost interest or found the task too difficult and gave up. It now read, *Doorman others Awning and Supply.* J. Brandon Yarlboro sold twine and to him, the combination of his product and awnings made perfect sense.

Stanley Doorman met him at the entrance to the store, greeted him warmly, and asked him to wait in his office while he finished with a customer. "It'll only take a minute," he explained before closing the door and returning to the sales floor.

Yarl took the interruption in stride. At the new employee orientation meeting Rupert Twain, managing partner of *Twain's Twine,* had explained the concept of *creative waiting.* "Look around," he told them, "find the clue that will break the awning business wide open." That's the way Rupert

Twain talked. "Our new line of balloon string will blow our competition out of the water," he would say enthusiastically as he smacked the podium with the palm of his hand. Or, "This years kite string will knock their socks off." Other string makers would be, "Clobbered, swept off their feet, or blown to smithereens." Landing the Doorman account would "Kick the door open" to every awning maker in the world.

Yarls was sure sales would "Shoot off the chart" if he could convince Stanley Doorman to use *Twain's Twine* on his awnings. At the end of every sales meeting Rupert Twain would rest his arms on the podium, look his sales team in the eye and ask, "How big can you think?"

In a corner of the room, under a stack of red and white striped canvas, Yarl saw the edge of a wooden board. After checking to make sure Stanley was still occupied, he pulled it loose. Attached to the board was a brass plaque. He ran his hand across the surface to clear away bits of cotton that had settled there.

"*To Stanley and Donald Doorman,*" he read, "*in appreciation for 22 years of*

continuous support of...."

A coffee stain covered the part of the plaque that told what the brothers had supported for twenty two years. He removed a handkerchief from his pocket, moistened it, and rubbed.

"You care about things," someone behind him said in a deep voice.

Thinking Stanley had finished with the customer and returned to his office Yarl stammered, "Excuse me Mr. Doorman but I saw the…" That's as far as he got because standing in front of him was not Stanley Doorman but a slightly overweight monk. His arms reached around his ample stomach and joined in clasped, pudgy fingers. A fringe of red hair circled the lower part of his head. His leather sandals were worn and cracked. He unclasped his hands long enough to pick a piece of lint from a sleeve of his brown canvas robe.

"Things," the monk repeated, "you care about them." He shrugged and added, "A personal observation."

"Excuse me?" was all Yarl could say.

"How about people?" the monk asked. "Do you care about people or just things?"

"Well sure," Yarl could feel himself getting mad at the stranger who'd entered the room without knocking and taken him by surprise. Besides, what kind of question is that to ask a person you've known for what? Ten seconds? "I care as much as the next guy."

"And," the monk unfolded his arms and held up an ink stained thumb. "What if the person next to you," he wiggled his thumb and pointed it at Yarl, "couldn't care less about people?"

"It's a figure of speech. I don't know who the guy next to me is but..." Yarl stopped and regrouped. "Wait a minute, why should I answer your questions?" He moved to within a foot of the monk, put his hands on his hips and asked, "Who are you?"

"Now we're getting somewhere," the monk said and threw an arm around Yarl's shoulders. "I'm Melvin," he explained as he moved to the window bringing Yarl with him. Once there, he pulled back a canvas curtain. "I belong to the order of monks out there." He pointed to a place outside the window.

For Yarl it was like looking through the wrong end of a telescope. Wooden buildings gave way to stone ones. Stone buildings faded into ones made with brick and mortar. Beyond the brick buildings was a tent and, under the tent, a group of monks, dressed like Melvin, sat around a picnic table.

It's like looking back through time, Yarl thought.

"It's like looking back through time isn't it?" Melvin asked.

It bothered Yarl that Melvin could read his thoughts.

"Does it bother you that I can read your thoughts?"

"No. Not at all," Yarl hated the idea that someone could figure out what he was thinking so easily.

"You've got to leave **that** behind." After he said it Melvin looked at Yarl and smiled.

"That? What's that? Or, what that are you talking about?" Being bombarded with questions had thrown Yarl off balance. His legs felt wobbly and his thinking confused.

"That," the monk replied and said slowly, "**T**hat **H**orrible **A**ttitude **T**hing. That **that**."

Yarl felt something in his chest break loose.

It was like pulling his foot from a shoe that had stuck in mud.

Or a loose tooth finally giving way.

Or footsteps in the snow… He could go on for hours finding ways to express what he was feeling. It was like the sound hair makes when it falls to the floor of a barber shop.

"Good," he heard Melvin say. "Your back. Now, let's talk about why I called you here."

Yarl started to tell him to hold on a second. **I** found the address for Doorman Brothers in the phone book. **I** made the appointment. And, if **I** land the account, **I'll** get credit for it. He was surprised to find he didn't want to waste time arguing over things that didn't matter.

He wanted to think big.

Melvin waited until he was sure he was listening. "With the passing of Donald Doorman, Stanley's brother, my order of monks is without, how shall I say it? A helper."

"You want me to volunteer to work with your organization?" Yarl interrupted thinking this was one of the keys to success Rupert Twain mentioned at the last sales meeting. "Get involved in the community," he'd encouraged them, "they buy from the people they know."

"In a way." Melvin paused. Yarl was the third salesman from Twain's Twine he'd interviewed and the only one to make it this far, it was time to take it to the next level. "Stanley Doorman supports our efforts by paying a modest salary. He provides office space and a phone. If you need paper clips or a staple puller, let him know."

Yarl started to say he wasn't looking for a job, he had one selling twine. He wanted to explain he was on the fast track to join the *Twain's Management Program.*

But he didn't.

"I'm going to tell you three things, then I'll join the other monks to make a few…adjustments. First, call me Mel, I've never been fond of Melvin."

Yarl nodded.

"Second, when the phone rings, pick it up. Don't say hello. Don't say goodbye. Just pick it up, press the yellow button on your desk, and hang up."

Yarl nodded.

"Third, welcome to the team and have a nice day."

Then he was gone. If it wasn't for the lingering smell of inexpensive canvas, Yarl wouldn't have known he'd been there.

The door to the office opened and Stanley Doorman entered. "Sorry to keep you waiting Yarl, it took longer than I thought."

"I, ah…" was all Yarl could say.

"I take it you met Mel," Stanley said, "and the fact that you're still here says things went well."

"I, ah…" was all Yarl could say.

Stanley picked up the *Twain's Twine* sample case, opened the door to his office and gestured for Yarl to follow him. They cut across the sales floor, past the display of an idea Stanley was trying out, awnings for inside the house. He stopped at a door that had "**Absolutely No Admittance!**" painted in black letters across a frosted glass panel, removed a key from his pocket, opened the door, and handed it to Yarl. "This is the only key to the room. Lose the key, lose the job," he said solemnly, "and break a million hearts. Do you understand what I'm saying?"

Yarl nodded he did but wasn't sure why. What job was he talking about? And how could he break a million hearts by losing a key?

"Have a nice day," Stanley said as he stepped out of the room and closed the door.

The office Yarl found himself in was the size of a janitor's closet. A gray metal desk was positioned in the center of the room. Behind the desk was a worn leather chair. On the desk was a phone and next to it, a yellow button.

He put his sample case in a corner, pulled the chair away from the desk, and sat down.

The phone rang.

He got up, opened the door, and looked for Stanley thinking the call was for him. He watched him enter his office and close the door.

The phone rang.

"Phone's ringing!" he called. He could see salespeople busy with customers but no one looked his way and told him to, "Take a number, I'll call them when I'm finished."

The phone rang.

He sat down in the chair and picked up the phone.

"Hello?" He whispered and it sounded more like a question than a greeting.

"This is Mel."

Yarl was relieved to hear a familiar voice. "Good it's you. The phone rang and I was afraid…"

Mel interrupted. "Do you remember the second thing I mentioned?"

Yarl's mind was spinning. Too much had gone on in too short a time. He'd come to *Doorman Brothers Awning and Supply* to sell twine, now he was sitting at a desk in a janitor's closet, talking to a monk on the telephone. He remembered call me Mel and something about having a nice day. Or a good day?

"I was afraid of that." There was a note of disappointment in Mel's voice. He'd read in a recent study the average person can remember two things and he'd given Yarl three. He'd hoped he was above average.

"Listen carefully," he said.

"Okay."

"Are you listening?"

"Okay."

"When the phone rings pick it up. Don't say hello. Don't say goodbye. Push the yellow button and hang up."

"Okay."

"Do you see the yellow button?"

"Okay."

"Have a nice day." His parting comment was followed by a buzz letting Yarl know he'd hung up.

Okay, Yarl thought as he put the phone on the cradle.

The phone rang.

He picked it up, held it for a few seconds, and hung up. "Nuts," he said to the empty room, "I forgot to press the yellow button."

The phone rang. He picked it up, pushed the yellow button but before hanging up he pressed the phone to his ear to find out who was calling, what they were calling about, and why he wasn't supposed to say anything.

"Hang up the phone Yarl," Mel said and he did.

Weekday mornings Yarl arrived at *Doorman Brothers Awning and Supply* at eight o'clock, waved to Stanley, pulled the key from his pocket, and opened the door to his office. He turned on the light, sat down in the leather chair, and poured coffee from his thermos into a complimentary *When It Comes To Awnings, We've Got You Covered* cup. Minutes after putting the thermos back in his lunch box the phone would ring and following Mel's instructions, he'd lift the phone from the cradle, push the yellow button, and hang up.

At five in the afternoon he'd turn off the lights, lock the door, and walk to the entrance where Stanley was waiting.

"Busy day?" Stanley would ask.

"Very busy," Yarl would say. Or "Extremely busy." Sometime he would nod and not say anything. As he stepped on the sidewalk, he heard the door lock behind him.

During his third week on the job Yarl wondered who would call this number. The phone rang, he picked it up but after pushing the yellow button, he listened.

He heard a child's voice. *"...and wish I wasn't so much taller than the kids my age. They make fun of me and..."*

He hung up the phone, crossed the sales floor, and entered Stanley's office.

Stanley was sitting behind his desk and looked like he was expecting him.

"Excuse me Stanley," Yarl hesitated, not sure how to ask the question without letting him know he'd listened to the wish request. "I accidentally..."

Stanley raised his eyebrows asking with the look how accidental it was but instead of

saying anything, he pointed to the window. Yarl crossed the room, pulled back the curtain, and looked out.

At the far end of the street, past the wooden buildings, and the stone ones. Beyond the buildings of brick and mortar, he saw the tent and beneath it monks sitting around the picnic table.

He started to ask why Stanley told him to look but before he did he glanced back and said, "Hold on, something's different. One of them is gone. There were six when I looked before, now there are five."

"Want to know where he went?" Stanley asked.

"Not really," was Yarl's first response that was immediately followed by, "Sure, who wouldn't."

"Yes or no Yarl." It was obvious Stanley was not in the mood to mess around.

"Yes," from Yarl.

Stanley stepped from behind his desk, removed a stack of canvas samples from a chair, and gestured for Yarl to sit down. He grabbed another chair, turned it around, and sat in front of him. This will be the hard part, he told himself, if he makes it through this he'll be okay. "The phone call from the kid who wished he wasn't so tall?" He checked to make sure Yarl was listening before finishing with, "That's where the monk went."

"I don't..." Yarl was confused.

Stanley started over. "The phone rings and you pick it up."

"Okay."

"It rings when a kid makes a wish."

Yarl thought for a moment before asking, "Here? In Stemsville?" He was referring to the city where he lived and *Doorman Brothers Awnings and Supply* was located.

"Think bigger."

"Ohio?"

"Bigger."

"The United States and the countries on its borders?" Yarl was grasping at bits of information still lingering in his mind from the geography class he'd taken his freshman year in high school.

"Bigger."

"Like, the world?" Yarl stammered.

Stanley nodded and said, "Like the world."

Yarl gasped. "And the yellow button?"

Stanley took Yarl's hand and lead him back to the window. "See the light bulb in the middle of the picnic table Monk Mel is pointing to?"

Yarl nodded he did.

"When you push the button on your desk, the light turns on and one of the monks leaves."

"To the person who called? The one making the wish?" Yarl asked.

Stanley smiled. Yarl was almost there. "To **help** the person on the phone making the wish."

Yarl walked to the door.

"Yarl," Stanley called after him.

He stopped with a hand on the door knob.

"That's why your job is so important." Stanley was out of his chair and standing with a hand on Yarl's shoulder. "No one picks up the phone. No one presses the button." He paused and shook his head before continuing. "No light goes on and no one leaves."

"And the child making the wish?" Yarl asked.

Stanley shook his head, letting Yarl know it would go unanswered.

Yarl stood by the door thinking about what Stanley said.

"And Yarl."

"Yes."

"Have a nice day," He said as he closed the door.

When Yarl got to his office he sat in his leather chair and thought of the wishes he'd made as a kid. He remembered the ache that went ahead of the wish. He thought of the kid that worried about being too tall. He pictured a monk flying off, or driving off, he was going to have to find out how the they traveled, how they knew where to go, crossing time zones, if they got travel pay, and..."

The phone rang. He picked it up and listened. "...*I wish I had a puppy. There aren't any kids in my neighborhood and...*"

He pushed the yellow button and thought of the light on the picnic table turning on. He pictured a monk standing and... what? He was gong to have to find out what they do after they stand up. Or if they stand up?

There was a lot he needed to learn about his job.

Yarl woke up in the middle of the night thinking of the refrigerator question; does the light inside stay on when the door is closed? Only in his case, does the phone in his office ring if there's no one there to answer it?

He got to *Doorman Brothers Awning and Supply* early the next morning and was surprised to find Stanley waiting at the door. Yarl gave him a look that asked what he was doing here so early? Stanley yawned, mumbled, "Don't ask," and shuffled away.

When Yarl opened the door to his office the air was heavy with the smell of canvas and Mel was sitting on his desk with his bare legs dangling over the side.

"You have questions?" Mel asked through a smile.

"Well, yea," Yarl answered then changed it to, "yes."

"About the monk thing?"

"Huh?" Mel had thrown a curve ball. The one thing he hadn't wondered about was the monk thing. Everything about Mel and the group around the picnic table said monk.

"We're not monks," Mel said matter-of-factly, "were wizards. Wish wizards to be exact.

Yarl couldn't think of what to say. If they weren't monks why did they wear brown canvas robes and sandals?

"I didn't think you'd believe me if I told you who we are up front, so saying we were monks seemed like a good place to start."

Yarl couldn't think of what to say.

"We help kids who wish. Their wish comes through the wish phone, which I must say is in very good hands." He hoped Yarl realized he'd paid him a compliment but from the look on his face, he doubted it. "You press the button on your desk and a wizard leaves. That's it."

"But I..." Yarl finally thought of something to ask.

"Have a nice day," Monk Mel said. Or Wizard Mel. Or...

And he was gone.

"But I..." Yarl had a question but couldn't remember what it was.

The phone rang. He reached across his desk, picked it up, pushed the yellow button, and hung up.

He glanced at his watch and saw five minutes had passed since Stanley Doorman opened the door to his store. Could he answer more calls, fulfill more wishes, if he came in earlier he wondered. At five? Or four?

Stanley Doorman entered the room and screwed a hook in the wall. Then he put another one opposite the first. He left and returned with a hammock made of canvas. He put the ends of the hammock over the hooks.

He smiled at Yarl, stepped out of the room, and closed the door.

From that moment on Yarl never left the room. Three times a day someone knocked on the door and when he opened it, they handed him a tray of food. He picked up the phone all hours of the day and night. Sometimes he listened but usually he didn't. The two or three seconds saved by not eavesdropping would allow for four maybe five extra wish calls a day which amounted to, he pulled a pencil and paper from the desk drawer and multiplied five times seven; thirty-five more calls a week. Minimum.

It turned out Stanley Doorman was a great awning salesman but a terrible businessman and soon *Doorman Brothers Awning and Supply* was bought by *Fletcher-Gruber Investors* who dropped everything from the Doorman Brothers product line except the awning part. They spun it off to a group of Chinese investors who got rid of the awning part, kept the store, and turned it into a restaurant.

Yarl was not aware of any of this. He didn't leave his office, afraid he'd miss a wish call if he did. What happened on the other side of the door was of no interest to him.

The restaurant was purchased by *Flounder Wealth Management*, whose plan was to move Yarl's office to a temporary location while they tore down the building that had been the home of *Doorman Brothers Awning and Supply* for twenty-five years and replaced it with the seven story *Flounder Tower*.

Yarl had just climbed out of his hammock and was ironing a shirt when Lou, owner of the restaurant, tapped on his door, opened it and said, "Excuse please but…" before he could finish Ken Flounder squeezed past him and entered the office.

He was short, wore an expensive suit, and was smoking a cigar. His coal black hair was held firmly in place with styling gel.

"Yarl, we meet at last," he said, grabbing Yarl's hand and shaking it enthusiastically. "Ken Flounder, managing partner of *Flounder Wealth Management*. I've heard so much about you, all good I might add." He followed the comment with a laugh. "I want you to know I plan to keep everything the way it is. Don't fix it if it ain't broke is my motto. Keep the ball rolling towards the pins. Don't mistake the forest for the trees." His voice was too big for the room and his gestures too broad for an audience that had dwindled to one since Lou, having failed in his attempt to introduce him, left.

Ken didn't wait for Yarl to answer.

"I've been told by a reliable source incoming calls are **OFF THE CHART**." He punched the air with the hand that held the cigar then grew serious. "Know this. I plan to tweak a few things. Trim the fat, clear out the deadwood, and make the shiny shoes of next years goals pinch your toes."

He didn't wait for Yarl to answer.

"I'll need a vision statement, a list of anticipated calls, and a graph showing a wish to fulfillment ratio. I intend to iron out the wrinkles, fast track expenditures, and eliminate duplication. In short, Wish Wizard Inc. is going to get lean and mean."

Yarl thought Ken had come to the wrong office. "I pick up the phone when it…"

"Starting today Sheila, my secretary, will monitor your calls to determine speed of service, customer satisfaction, and means of payment." He walked to the door, spun around and smacked Yarl's desk with his fist. Speaking through cigar smoke he said, "We're going to incorporate. We're going to innovate. We're going online, joining the social network, and bloging. Let the word go out that from this day forward, *Wish Wizard's Inc.* will become a profit center. A critical piece of the growing *Flounder Wealth Management* empire."

Yarl expected Ken Flounder to use words like "Cut the competition off at the knees with our personalized service."

Or, "Smack them upside the head with our home page." He wondered if Ken Flounder had ever worked for Rupert Twain.

"Wishes," he said with a laugh as he left the room, "who knew you could charge for them?"

For a year after leaving his tiny office at *Doorman Brothers Awnings and Supply*, Yarl shared a cubicle with the sales manager of *Flounder Automotive*, a division of *Flounder Wealth Management*. He was asked to answer the phone when the manager was busy with a customer. That stopped when, out of a habit from years of working with Wish Wizards Inc., he picked up the phone, waited a second, and hung up.

When construction was finished, he was moved to the fourth floor of *Flounder Tower*, his own office, and the memo.

To: The staff of Wish Wizards, Inc.

From: Ken Flounder CEO, CFO, COO.

Subject: Downsizing

Your numbers are headed for the dumpster.

Get them up or get out.

Working together for a better tomorrow.

Your partner in the pursuit of wealth,

K. Flounder

Yarl put his arms on his desk, his head on his arms and sighed, "I wish I knew what to do."

He looked up when he heard the thump of a box dropped on his desk and was surprised to see an older Mel. The fringe of hair that circled his head had turned gray. The bottom of his canvas robe was frayed and he was leaning on Yarl's desk, trying to recover from carrying the box up four flights of stairs.

"Mel," Yarl shouted, got up, and gave the Monk/Wizard a hug. "What's this stuff?" he asked as he lifted a flap on top of the box and looked inside. He saw stacks of official looking documents describing monthly activity and long range plans.

He removed a folder with, "*Monthly Report Of Wish Wizards, Inc, a Division of Flounder Wealth Management*, printed across the front. The cover sheet was followed by a pie chart and graph with a line that started in the lower left corner of the page and rose steadily as it traveled to the right.

Yarl leafed through the document. The heading on the last page read:

<u>Report Summary.</u>

"*Calls:* Up.

Call to action ratio: 1.

Customer Satisfaction: + 4 .

Outlook: Optimistic."

It was signed, J. Brandon Yarlboro, DM (dispatch manager.)

"I didn't write this," Yarl protested. "I didn't do the research. It would take months of work and with the phone calls…"

Mel waited for him to finish before whispering, "He doesn't read them."

"But…" from Yarl.

"You put it here." Mel took the report from Yarl and placed it in his out basket.

"Okay," Yarl said.

"Robin, the mail person takes it from your basket and gives it to Sheila who puts a check mark in a box next to *Wish Wizards, Inc. Monthly Report* and files it."

Yarl nodded, mentally following the report from his desk to Sheila and finally, the file cabinet.

Mel continued. "On his way to lunch, Ken Flounder calls Sheila and asks if the monthly reports are in. She checks her list and says yes. Or, maybe the *Off Shore Drilling Division* is late."

"That's it?" Yarl asked.

"For this month," Mel gestured to the box on Yarl's desk, "and the rest of the year."

He patted Yarl on the shoulder, told him to, "Have a nice day," and was gone.

Later that morning, Ken Flounder leaned in his office and said enthusiastically, "Top notch report this month Yarl. Sheila tells me it was turned in on time. Keep up the good work and you'll retire a wealthy man." Ken Flounder started down the hall.

"Mr. Flounder," Yarl called.

Ken sighed. He was on his way to the new employee meeting and was running late. "Yes Yarl?" he said impatiently.

"Have a nice day sir."

"Well thank you Yarl," Ken answered as he hurried away.

Yarl leaned back in his worn leather chair, put his sandaled feet on top of his gray metal desk and said softly, "I am a wealthy man."

The phone on his desk rang and another day at Wish Wizard, Inc. had begun.

Chapter 2
Stupid Nameover

Fenton Alowishus Tug was mad.

The more he thought about it the madder he got and he'd been thinking about it since afternoon recess.

Halfway through supper he threw his napkin on the table and stomped out of the room.

His mother asked, "Do you think it's the meat loaf?"

His father patted her hand and told her, "I'll talk to him when he's had a chance to cool off."

His older brother Felix looked across the table, pointed with his fork and said, "If he's not coming back can I have his dessert?"

Fenton slammed the door to his room.

"Why can't I have a normal name?" he moaned. "Why can't I have a name like Brian or Andy? Nobody makes fun of kids with names like that."

He sat down in his chair, put his arms on his desk, rested his chin on his arms, and thought about recess.

They were playing kickball. it was a close game, and he was up. The bases were loaded and all he had to do was get the ball out of the infield and the winning run would cross the plate.

"Slow and smooth," he hollered to the pitcher, a perfect call for the kind of kick he needed to put the game away.

The ball came the way he asked. He turned slightly to his left, drew back his foot, and planned to kick it over the shortstops head when he heard the fans of the other team chant:

"Fenton Tug
Is a funny little guy,
We can't pronounce his middle name
so we won't even try."

"Every time," he moaned, "at a crucial moment in a game or when I'm at the chalk board and Ms Chalmer asks a really hard question I hear them whisper:

"Tug old boy
don't look so bleak
you'll think of the answer
if it takes all week."

"Then I forget about the game, the ball, the question, everything except what a stupid name I have and why I can't have a name over."

He sat up when the thought came to him and he realized the answer had been there all the time. You can ask for a "do over" in kickball if you don't like the way the ball came to you so why can't you ask for a "name over" if you don't like the name you were given?

He laughed out loud and wondered why he hadn't thought of it before. Why can't I choose a new one? Why do I have to keep the name I have?

He closed his eyes and said in a loud voice, **"I WISH I HAD A DIFFERENT NAME!"**

The room was quiet when he finished, then someone coughed.

He opened his eyes.

A man his grandfather's age, wearing a wrinkled gray sweat suit was leaning against the wall next to the closet. He wore leather sandals with no socks, was completely bald, and looked like he hadn't shaved in a week. Doughnut crumbs trailed across the front of his sweatshirt where **W.W. Inc. dot com** was printed in blue letters. After the **dot com**, he saw something that looked like the wishbone of a turkey.

"What's your wish kid?" The tone of the stranger's voice suggested he'd been doing whatever he did for a long time and didn't enjoy doing it anymore.

"Who are you?" Fenton knew the rules about talking to strangers, but they were for those you met on the street or at the mall, not one who shows up in your room.

"I'm a wish wizard," the visitor answered through a yawn. "Actually a retired wish wizard but there's been an increase in wishes since the company went online," he pointed to the front of his sweatshirt, "so they called me in to help with the overload." He raised his arms above his head and bent forward, attempting to touch his toes.

He glanced at his watch, "Better get a move on, I have to get to a birthday party in Scranton before she blows out the candles."

"I've wished before and no one's come," Fenton didn't like being surprised and he was still mad about the kids in his class making fun of his name.

"Look Fenton, I don't have time to argue with you but to set the record straight, you haven't *wished* you've *wanted*." While he talked the wish wizard pulled a battered notebook from the back pocket of his sweatpants. "According to our records, you *wanted* a different name on November 21 & 23. Then in December...," he turned the page, studied it for a moment, and looked at Fenton. "You asked Santa for a different name?"

Fenton shrugged and looked at the top of his shoes before recovering enough to say, "Big deal, want or wish, they're the same aren't they?" He wasn't about to get caught on a technicality while talking to a retired wish wizard who'd been called in at the last minute because all the other wizards were busy.

"Oh there's a big difference where I come from." The wish wizard shook his head as he spoke, amazed someone Fenton's age hadn't learned the difference between the two words. "You want a game or toy, and if you don't get it, you want a cheeseburger for lunch. Or you want to go to the movies with your friend Billy Gilsky. When the movies over you, want to go to his house for a sleep over.

"But to wish for something," he paused, pulled back the curtain and looked out the window before saying, "you don't switch around. You wish for the same thing in the morning and afternoon for days and weeks. Do you see the difference?"

Fenton nodded.

The wish wizard glanced at his watch. "You've got three minutes kid. It's time to wish or cut bait."

Fenton came to the conclusion that a retired wish wizard on a tight schedule doesn't mess around.

"Okay, I wish I had a different name." After he said it he closed his eyes and scrunched up his face thinking that's what you did when making a wish with a wish wizard standing by the window in your room. The next thing you know you have a new name.

"Impressive but that's not how it works." The wish wizard must have gotten a cramp in a calf muscle because he stuck his left leg behind him and pressed his hands against the wall.

Fenton opened his eyes.

"I wished for a name over!" He could feel himself getting mad. Didn't anyone understand how easy it could be? One minute your Fenton and the next you're...what? Well, you're whatever name the wish wizard gives you.

"Sorry but that's not in my job description," the wish wizard shook his head and made Fenton wonder if he'd read his thoughts or if he'd said, "whatever name the wish wizard gives you," out loud. "I don't pick names for kids. They're not happy when I do and it takes too much time which, by the way," he pointed to his watch, "you don't have much of."

He crouched next to Fenton. "I'm only going to say this once." Fenton perked up. He could tell by the tone in the wish wizard's voice he'd given this explanation before, maybe dozens of times to other kids who wanted their name changed. Maybe this was his specialty, Fenton thought. Maybe that's why they called him in on such short notice instead of sending someone else. And maybe, just maybe, he wasn't going to a birthday party in Scranton but to help a girl who wasn't happy with her name.

Fenton's thoughts were interrupted when he realized the wish wizard was talking. "...you say, I wish my name was Ronald, or Donald, then I wave my wand in a circle," as he talked he rummaged around in a battered canvas bag and pulled out a bent metal rod that looked like a bicycle spoke with a ball on one end, "aim this at you, say something magical, and I'm on my way to Scranton. Got it?"

The wish wizard straightened and said solemnly, "The clock's ticking kid, make your wish."

Fenton's face flushed with anger. **"I wish I had a stupid nameover. I wi..."** He was going to say something about how all the good names were probably taken and why couldn't the wish wizard get it through his thick head he didn't know what name he wanted and if he expected him to pick one he should at least let him know which ones were available?

Before he could, the wish wizard mumbled, "Close enough." He heard something pop and when the smoke cleared, he was gone.

What Fenton didn't know was the moment he heard the pop, his name in the attendance book in Ms Chalmer's third grade class was changed, as well as the name taped to his lunch box, and stenciled on his backpack.

His old name had been erased and a new one had taken its place in the mind of Mr. Logan, the principal of Buffalo Bill Cody Elementary, his classmates, and their parents.

Everything with his name written on it, every person who had his name locked in their memory, and every scrap of paper no matter how small that had Fenton, or Alowishus, or Tug on it, was instantly changed to, **Stupid Nameover**.

That's the way it goes when dealing with a retired wish wizard who'd been called in because the other wizards were busy and only had fifteen minutes to spare.

"Get in," was the wish wizard's motto, "fulfill a wish, and get out."

The next morning his mother opened the door to his room, leaned in and said, "Time to get up Stupid." She didn't laugh when she said it. She didn't hesitate as if trying to remember his name.

"That's odd," Fenton mumbled as he climbed out of bed.

At the breakfast table his father put the newspaper he was reading down and asked, "Busy day at school today Stupid?"

His older brother walked in the kitchen and said, "Morning mom. Morning dad." He popped Fenton on the head with his knuckle and said, "Morning Stupid," as he walked behind his chair.

Normally Fenton would duck or swat his brother's hand away.

Normally his father would tell him to, "Take it easy on the little guy."

And normally his mother would get upset and say, "If he turns out to be stupid it's going to be your fault."

But no one said anything because when it's your name, being called Stupid is no big deal.

Maybe it wasn't the best name in the world. Maybe if the wish wizard had more time he could have come up with something more traditional. But, on the other hand, there wasn't much the kids at school could do to make it worse.

He'd wished for a new name and got one. It wasn't exactly what he had in mind but it was better than his old one.

He picked up his lunch box and was relieved when he saw **Stupid** written on the handle.

At school Ms Chalmer called on him to answer the first question of the morning. "Stupid," she said, "can you tell us what kind of triangle this is?"

There was no laughter when she said his name.

There was no whispering behind his back.

His classmates didn't ask their teacher if she really expected someone named Stupid to know anything about triangles.

He relaxed and thought maybe his new name wasn't so bad. Maybe in a few days he'd get use to it. And maybe, when he heard the kids in his class call him Stupid, he'd know they were saying his name and not talking about how dumb he was.

The rest of the morning flew by and before he knew it, it was time for recess.

Kickball was the game again today and, as he walked from the dugout to home plate, he was faced with the same situation as yesterday. There were runners on base and all he had to do was kick a little blooper over the third baseman's head and the victory celebration would begin.

"Fast and bouncy," he hollered and went into his pre-kick routine. He tapped home plate with the heal of his right foot, tugged on the cuff of his jeans, and took two steps back so he could get a short run before stepping into the ball.

The pitcher rolled the ball the way he wanted.

He saw it coming towards him, pulled his right leg back and froze when he heard the fans of the other team yell,

"They changed his clothes
they changed his name,
but they made a mistake
when they put Stupid in the game."

The ball bounced off his leg and dribbled along the foul line toward third base.

He made no effort to run.

He was too stunned to move.

The pitcher scooped up the ball before it went out of bounds and tossed it to first.

He was out and the game was over.

He stood on home plate after the bell rang calling the students back to class. He worked his way across the infield, stepped over the left field foul line, and started up the path to school.

"I wish I knew what was going on," he muttered as he walked along with his hands jammed in his pockets and his head down.

Someone coughed.

He turned and was surprised to see the retired wish wizard sitting on the bench beside the picnic table.

"Long time no see," the wish wizard said.

It's the same guy who was in my room yesterday, Fenton thought. Or was it the day before? He couldn't remember. He's wearing the same clothes, the same sandals, and has the same canvas bag with the magic wand in it next to him on the bench.

"Sup?" The wish wizard asked.

Fenton looked puzzled.

"Hey," the wish wizard said, "just because I'm retired doesn't mean I'm out of the loop. I hear the way kids talk."

Fenton sat down on the bench and mumbled, "They made fun of my old name and they made fun of my new one." He stopped talking, afraid if he said another word he'd start to cry.

"Changing *your* name doesn't change *them*," the wish wizard said softly and put a comforting hand on his shoulder. "You could have chosen a letter or number, it wouldn't have made any difference." The wish wizard paused to let Fenton think about what he'd said before adding, "They'd find something to make fun of."

"But if it's not my name, why do they do it?" Fenton's voice cracked and he used the sleeve of his sweater to rub away a tear that had started down his cheek.

"It's what kid's do," the wish wizard shrugged and repeated, "it's just what kids do." He shook his head hoping to convey it was a fact of life for someone Fenton's age.

As they sat together on the wooden bench it slowly dawned on Fenton, if a persons name didn't make any difference, if he could have chosen a letter or a number and the fans of the other team would still make fun of him, maybe he didn't have to keep his new name. Maybe he could get his old name back before some kid talking to a wish wizard in Milwaukee claimed it.

It took him a few minutes to figure it out and a few more to work up the courage to ask if he could have his old name back.

Silence followed his question and for a moment he thought the wish wizard had dozed off. Or hadn't heard him. Or worse yet, was ignoring him.

He said a little louder, "I wish I had my old name back."

"That was quick." The wish wizard said as he rummaged through his canvas bag. "Are you sure you don't want to talk it over? Spend some time discussing the difference between want and wish?"

Fenton thought for a retired wish wizard he had a pretty good memory.

The wish wizard picked at a spot of dried mustard stuck to the top of the picnic table with the end of his wand. "I've got some time on my hands. I don't have to be in Denver for another hour, a high school freshman is asking a girl to the homecoming dance."

"No," Fenton cried out. "I've learned something important and I think, no I'm sure, I want my name back." He held up his hand, cutting the wizard off. "I know how it works. I wish for the name I want and you do something with your wand."

He spoke quickly because he couldn't wait another second to switch things back to the way they were.

He closed his eyes, scrunched up his face even though he knew he didn't have to and said, "I wish for the name of Fenton Alowishus Tug."

When nothing happened he opened one eye, looked at the wish wizard, and added, "Please."

He heard the wish wizard say, "There you go. Or is it there I go? I get those two…"

He heard a pop and when he opened his eyes, he discovered he was alone. "Is that it?" he asked the empty place on the picnic bench where the wish wizard had been sitting.

"Fenton?" someone called.

"Fenton," someone repeated. "Time to get up dear, it's a school day. This is the second time I've called you." When his mother saw he was awake she hurried down the hall to his brother's room.

He jumped out of bed, ran to his desk, and checked the name on his backpack. He smiled when he saw **Tug** stenciled above the pocket that held his pencils.

He ran downstairs and into the kitchen. He relaxed when he saw **Fenton** printed on the handle of his lunch box.

His father put the newspaper down and asked, "Busy day at school today Fenton?"

Had he dreamed it, he wondered, about the retired wish wizard, his wand, and the nameover? Or had it really happened?

His older brother came to the breakfast table and said, "Morning mom. Morning dad." Then he popped Fenton on the head with his knuckle and said, "Morning stupid."

Fenton checked the name on his lunch box to make sure, then said confidently, "Not today Felix. I'm not stupid today."

Chapter 3
EAR ISLAND

Fenton Alowishus Tug was mad when he walked in the kitchen.

His mother told him, "You get them from your father's side of the family."

His father lowered the newspaper and said, "Don't worry, you'll outgrow them."

His brother suggested he wear a stocking cap.

Fenton wondered why he couldn't look like the other kids in his class. Nobody made fun of Brian Alexander's ears.

It happened on the playground during afternoon recess. Fenton was the last kicker in a scoreless game. "Slow and bouncy," he'd yelled and the pitcher rolled the ball the way he asked.

He looked at the gap between the third baseman and the foul line. The other team had gone into the "Tug Shift," a move that pulled the fielders towards first base. He imagined the ball blasting off his foot, sailing over third base, and not stopping until it came to rest under the picnic table by the left field foul line. He could hear the cheers of his teammates as he rounded the bases.

What he actually heard was a chant from the fans of the other team:

"Me oh my oh
Fenton Tug,
his ears stick out
like handles on a jug."

He was so embarrassed he couldn't move and watched helplessly as the ball rolled past his poised right foot.

The catcher tagged him with the ball, yelled "You're out," and the game was over.

When the school day finally came to an end and the bus reached his stop, he got off and ran to his house.

He slammed the front door as he came in and stomped up the stairs.

He slammed the door to his room and then opened it and slammed it again.

He fell across his bed, his face red with anger. "I wish my ears weren't so big," he moaned between sobs.

His outburst was followed by silence then someone belched.

He looked up embarrassed, he thought he was the only one in the room.

"You don't have an antacid tablet do you?" The stranger asked. "Tums? Rolaids? Dr. Pepper?"

Sitting in the chair by his desk was a heavy set, middle aged woman. She wore white sweat pants that stopped at her knees and a black tee shirt with *Sneed Family Reunion '79* printed across the front. Her hair was pulled together and held in place by a rubber band creating what looked to Fenton like a fountain erupting from the top of her head. Her orange socks disappeared into a pair of scuffed white deck shoes.

A worn canvas bag rested against a leg of the chair.

She was leaning forward with her elbows on her knees. "I tell them I need an hour after I eat before I do a wish gig, and what do I get? Twenty minutes." She looked at Fenton, gave a half smile, and said apologetically, "It's not your fault kid, it's a scheduling problem."

She held her head in her hands and the pained look on her face suggested she was experiencing acute abdominal distress. "7-Up? Ginger Ale? Anything?"

"Who are you?" Fenton finally worked up the courage to ask, curiosity pushing his personal problems aside.

She rolled her eyes and took a deep breath before saying, "Let's see if we can figure this out, okay?" There was a touch of sarcasm in her voice. "You came in your room crying…"

"I wasn't crying," he interrupted.

"Oh, right. Sorry." She held up her hands, letting him know she meant no offense. "You came in your room *extremely upset*?"

He nodded he was okay with that.

"You slammed the door and threw yourself on the bed." She raised her eyebrows and asked, "With me so far?"

He nodded he was.

"You made a **wish** and I show up." She leaned toward him and asked, "Does any of this sound familiar?" She belched again. "Chewing gum? Throat lozenge? Breath mint?"

"I have a caramel," Fenton volunteered.

"Hand it over. If it works, you can tell the world you found the cure for an upset stomach." She removed the wax paper and popped the caramel in her mouth.

"You're a wish wizard?" Fenton hadn't had much experience with wish wizards, he'd only met one, but he'd been more, well, normal looking.

She touched her finger to her nose indicating he was right. "In the flesh," she said as she chewed the caramel.

"What about the other guy? Bald, sandals and ah, retired. He said he was a retired wish wizard."

"Rodney?" She pulled a black book from the canvas bag and Fenton saw, **Wish Wizard, Inc. Work Schedule,** printed on the front in gold letters. "Let's see, ah, hear you go. He's taking some time off," she mumbled as she turned a page, "in Phoenix, at a skateboard convention."

"He's not available?" There was a hint of panic in Fenton's voice.

She looked at her book and flipped a few more pages. "Not until Tuesday." She stood. "It's your wish Fenton, if you want to wait for Rodney that's okay with me. I'll go home, I could use a nap."

"No, no. It's just that I know him and…that's okay, you're fine. Sorry," Fenton started to touch her hand but felt embarrassed by a show of affection for someone he'd just met.

"No harm no foul," she said and sat down. "Besides I think the caramel helped. Now," she said as she removed a pad of paper and a wooden pencil from the bag. After checking to make sure the point on the pencil wasn't broken she looked at Fenton and asked, "What seems to be the problem?"

"What seems…" He couldn't believe someone could be so dense. "Isn't it obvious? Look at my ears!" He was embarrassed telling her. He'd never actually said it out loud before, at least when someone was listening.

She grabbed his chin, turned his head from side to side, and looked puzzled. "Like I said, what's the problem?"

"Are you blind?" Fenton pulled away, put his hands on his hips, and stomped his foot. "It's my ears. They're too big. They stick out too far. They…"

She interrupted, not sure how long he could go before exhausting the list of reasons he'd been storing up for years. "Your ears look fine," she said as she raised her hands in the air and twisted from side to side. "I've got to find a different job, my back's killing me. One minute I'm home eating chicken noodle soup and the next thing I know, I'm in a kids room inspecting his ears. No heads up to let me know what's going on. No warning. Just boom and I'm here."

She took a deep, calming breath, leaned forward, and said so quietly he almost missed it, "It's not your ears, it's where you live."

"I don't get it. How does where I live have anything to do with my ears?" He was lost. What she said made no sense to him.

"Right," she said as she rummaged through her canvas bag, eventually producing a small wooden box. Whoever painted it hadn't scraped away the old, cracked paint before applying a new coat. He could see blue dots and dashes circling the lid.

"Sorry, wrong box," she said and plunged her hand back in the bag. After what seemed to Fenton like hours of pushing things around, she produced a box that looked exactly like the first one. She removed the lid, took a pinch of green powder from inside, and flicked it in Fenton's direction.

The last thing he heard the wish wizard say was, "I don't remember it being that shade of green."

A cool breeze blew across Fenton's face and the air had a salty taste.

He opened his eyes and saw he was standing on a playground surrounded by water that stretched as far as he could see.

He glanced towards the bleachers and saw the wish wizard who'd been in his room, holding a bag of popcorn, surrounded by dozens of kids.

She gave him the thumbs up sign.

"Where are we?" He mouthed the words knowing he couldn't be heard above the roar of the crowd and the sound of the waves breaking on the edge of the playground.

She nodded she understood and pointed to the scoreboard in center field. "***Welcome to Ear Island***," was printed in large letters and below it he saw, **"*Home of the Ear Canals-We Will, We Will, Wax You.*"**

He looked down and saw. **"*Ear Canals,*"** printed on the front of his purple T-shirt. And, though he couldn't see it, ***TUG*** was written on the back in lime green letters. Below his name was the number one.

He discovered he was standing on home plate. He started to call for the pitcher to roll the ball fast and bouncy but stopped, his mouth moving but no sound coming out. Brian Alexander, his nemesis from school, was the pitcher. At least, he thought it was Brian. His ears looked like giant funnels, wide on the ends then tapering to a point where they connected to his head.

"What's going on?" Fenton muttered.

He glanced at third base. Was that Brian's buddy Andy, leaning forward, ready to pounce on anything kicked his way? Fenton wasn't sure how well he could pounce with ears the size of footballs.

He looked at the crowd in the bleachers and they had big ears. Some looked like cauliflower. Some were the size of large ripe tomatoes. Or zucchini. Or butternut squash.

The odd thing was no one in the stands or on the field seemed to notice.

He moved his hands hesitantly to his ears afraid of what he might find. He relaxed when he discovered they were small and smooth, the same size they were when the wish wizard showed up in his room.

He shook his head trying to clear his thoughts of anything that would keep him from concentrating on the game. "Fast and bouncy," he shouted to the pitcher and in case he couldn't hear, he gestured with his hand.

Brian's funnel ears flopped up and down when he nodded he got it. The players on the infield slid toward first base leaving a gaping hole between the third baseman and the foul line.

Fenton tingled with excitement. This is it he thought. Then, in a bold, un-Fenton like move, he pointed to the left field fence, signaling that's where he was going to kick the ball. He tapped the plate with his right foot, touched the cuff of his trousers, stepped back two paces, and drew back his leg.

Everyone in the bleachers stood, except for the wish wizard, who was eating a hotdog and sipping a diet coke. The crowed chanted:

"Fenton Tug
hear our cheers
if they can make it to your brain
through your tiny little ears."

The ball, rolling toward him, began to blur, cleared up, then blurred again. The sound of the crowd faded, rose in volume, then dropped to a whisper.

He looked desperately to the wish wizard for an explanation of what was happening.

She shrugged and lifted her shoulders as if to say she had no idea.

He swung his foot where he thought the ball would be but instead of hearing the smack of his shoe against rubber he heard a thump.

He opened his eyes and saw the wish wizard's canvas bag halfway across the room.

"Nice kick kiddo," she said as she struggled to get out of the chair. "Well, I've gotta scoot. A message on my beeper says I'm needed in Fargo. Some kid…"

"No. Hold on. You can't go yet.," Fenton protested. The kid in Fargo could wait, he needed answers now. "What's the point? The last time there was a point, a reason for what happened."

"Sorry," she said through a forced smile, "I don't do points."

She stood, straightened her T-shirt and said, "Unless, about your ears…"

"Yes," Fenton said, wondering if he would be able to remember what she told him or if he should find a pencil and write it down.

"I've seen worse." She patted his cheek fondly, grunted when she picked up her canvas bag, stepped out of his room, and closed the door.

Fenton sat on the edge of his bed and thought. On the playground at school they made fun of him because his ears were too big. On Ear Island, they made fun of him because they were too small. What was it the wish wizard said about the problem being where he lived?

Fenton laid back and thought some more.

The next morning things at the Tug house were running late because the alarm hadn't gone off and everyone had overslept.

Fenton only had enough time to grab a piece of toast and pick up his lunch box.

"You look nice," his mother said and touched his cheek.

His father lowered the newspaper, told him, "Don't worry about the you know whats," and pointed to his ears.

Fenton dashed out the door before his brother came to the breakfast table.

Brian and Andy were just getting on the school bus when Fenton rounded the corner half a block away. He took off at a dead run hoping to get there before the doors closed. As he got closer he heard a window slide down.

"Don't run too fast Dumbo," he heard Brian's yell as he sped by, "with ears as big as yours you might take off."

Andy, Brian's seat mate, was still laughing when Fenton got on. Brian brought his hands to his ears and flapped them up and down. Andy laughed so hard he almost fell off the seat.

"Where we headed today Fenton?" Mr. Fleener, the bus driver, asked each kid the same question as they got on.

"Drop me off at Ear Island before taking the other kids to school?" Fenton told him.

"Boys," Mr. Fleener looked in the curved mirror over his head and spoke directly to Brian and Andy. "We can't leave for Ear Island until you close your window."

Fenton smiled and took a seat at the front of the bus. "If only," he said under his breath and repeated for good measure, "if only."

Chapter 4
FINE PRINT

Fenton Alowishus Tug wondered why he had to be the only one in his family who wore glasses? And why he was the only kid in Ms Chalmer's class to need them?

Why couldn't he have perfect eyesight like Brian Alexander? No one made fun of kids who don't wear glasses.

He was tired of being teased about them by fans of the opposing team. At a crucial moment In yesterday's kickball game, with two outs and runners at first and third, he'd stepped to the plate a focused kicker. Before the first pitch, before he could tell the pitcher how he wanted the ball rolled to him, the fans of the other team yelled:

"Look at Fenton,
Alowishus
his glasses are as big
as dinner dishes."

To make matters worse his own team, **HIS OWN TEAM**, joined in:

"Count his eyes,
two, three four,
he couldn't see the ball
if he had two more."

He ran past the bleachers filled with classmates laughing and pointing at him. He went to the far corner of the playground where a picnic table had been placed beneath a tree planted the year Buffalo Bill brought his wild west show to Stemsville.

He put his arms on the table, his chin on his arms, and thought about yesterday's game.

Not wanting to hear their corny cheers, he put his glasses in his lunch box before jogging to his position in right field. He could see the grass beneath his feet but the first baseman was a blur and home plate a distant memory.

Once in position, he started his usual outfield chatter and hoped he was facing the right direction. *"C'mon Lenny,"* he hollered and clapped his hands. *"No kicker Lenny baby. No kicker at the plate. Way to go Lennnnyyy."*

He was about to start through his chatter routine a second time when the ball smacked him in the chest and bounced toward the foul line. The force of the blow knocked him off his feet and he ended up crawling on his hands and knees, hoping to find the ball before the runner reached third base. As he searched the fans of both teams yelled;

> **"Put on his glasses,**
> **lift him from the dirt,**
> **put him in the dugout**
> **so he won't get hurt."**

He looked up in time to see Rudy "Big Foot" Griggs step on third base and turn for home, pointing triumphantly to someone in the crowd.

After yesterday's blunder and today's embarrassment, he decided he'd never play kickball again. From now on he'd stay inside during recess and work arithmetic problems . He sighed and mumbled, "I wish I didn't have to wear these stupid glasses."

He felt someone tug on the sleeve of his sweater. "Excuse please, but I would at this time be looking for a Fenton something Tug person whose name in the middle I cannot pronounce. Excusing please a second time for what I am sure is an unexpected eruption."

"You mean interruption, don't you?" Fenton spun around expecting to see someone had followed him from the playground to pile on more abuse.

"Probably, yes, most probably you are correct in selecting from all the words available that particular one. Such a command the young person I am talking to has of language. But as to the, ah, thing I was thinking?"

"Question?"

"Most probably sir, undoubtedly, but my question, thanking you if it is not too late for your assistance in providing the exact word I was looking at. Do you personally contain knowledge of this Tug person?"

"I'm Fenton Tug."

"Indeed you are. Oh most of a wonderful indeed. You," the visitor said as he folded a piece of paper and stuck it in his back pocket, "are undoubtedly him."

Fenton pushed his glasses in place to get a better look at the stranger.

Standing next to him was a young man whose head barely reached the top of the picnic table. He wore high top sneakers with no socks, short pants made from bib overalls, and a purple and white warm up jacket with *Wish Wizards Inc.* embroidered on the front. Inside the circle formed by the words, he saw the wishbone of a turkey. His shaggy brown hair stuck out from beneath a ball cap worn with the bill turned to the back. A button pinned to his jacket said, *"Celebrate Something!"*

"You're a wish wizard?" Fenton had never seen anyone, let alone a wish wizard, that looked like him.

"Most yesingly, Mr. Fenton sir, but not quite." He pulled himself to his full height and his head rose an inch above the top of the picnic table. He brought his right hand to his forehead in a clumsy salute and announced with pride, "I am almost an apprentice sir and you, Mr. Fenton with the glasses thing on your face, are precisely something like my first person to be wizarding."

Fenton noticed he was wearing a backpack jammed with an instrument for measuring wind speed, tongs for lifting blocks of ice, a golf club, a rake, and a bicycle pump.

The almost apprentice wish wizard noticed Fenton looking at his backpack and anticipating his question answered, "$29.95 sir. It would be slightly used by an almost apprentice before my purchase of it."

"What…I…you." Fenton struggled to connect what he'd been thinking with what the visitor said.

"The Almost Apprentice Kit Level 1 sir," he said proudly. "But the book in the $29.95 kit says, if I could find it, that I should tell you Sheldon." He rummaged through the backpack, produced a name tag, pealed the paper off the back, and stuck it on the front of his jacket. *"Hi,"* it said, *"am I Sheldon?"*

Fenton could feel himself getting angrier by the second. For an average kid with a simple arithmetic problem like how much three plus seven is, maybe an almost apprentice wish wizard would be okay. But for him, Fenton Alowishus Tug, a kid with a real problem involving glasses and classmates making fun of him for wearing them, there was definitely **NO APPRENTICE WAY!**

"Sheldon," Fenton said politely.

"I am most attentively listening as you speak words from your mouth Mr. Fenton sir." Sheldon inched closer, anxious to learn what he'd been sent to do.

"Well, that's the problem." Fenton stood. He could see kids leaving the playground and walking back to the school building. "I was kidding about being Fenton. I'm really, ah, Norman, yeah that's it, Norman Shenkel, and I'd love to stay out her and talk but I've got to go to class." To make sure Sheldon understood, he pointed in the direction of the school.

Rather proud that he'd been able to think of an excuse so quickly, Fenton, now known to Sheldon as Norman, smiled as he left for his classroom.

"A thousand apologies Mr. Norman sir, if that exact number seems adequate for what one would think if one thought about it. My mistake has caused, it seems, an embarrassment to yourself and, if I may be allowed to say so, me as well. It says in the front of the starter kit book thing, you only have one chance to make a good impersonation. I'm sure you understand my painfulness in committing such a grievous error. If however you would please **not** at this moment or the next, call the *1-800-WIZ-ARDS* number written on the business card I have not given you because they cost me personally $12.00 for a hundred. The cards are used and have the name of another almost apprentice on them but the telephone number at or near the bottom doesn't care.

"My mentor Mr. Clifford," Sheldon spook louder as Fenton hurried away, "would certainly, if informed, not be pleased, or for that matter, happy with my first effort to contact a wish person and in doing so addressing, it appears, the wrong one.

I am profusely embarrassed by my conduct. Most profusely indeed."

Fenton glanced back to see if Sheldon was following him and discovered he was, if you could call it that. His short legs made him waddle from side to side like a penguin walking across a patch of ice. He staggered under the weight of the backpack that pulled him sideways and the odd collection of instruments banged together with each step he took.

He saw Sheldon twice during the afternoon. Once when he glanced up from a problem in his arithmetic workbook and saw the top of a rake go by the window at the back of the room.

The second was when he heard mumbling in the hallway, watched the door to his room open and saw Mrs. Thrum, the school secretary, with one hand on Sheldon's shoulder and the other pointing at him. He slid down in his seat but knew Sheldon had found him and, in the process, discovered he'd lied about who he was.

"….and Fenton." He'd been so involved in what was going on at the door, he hadn't heard what the Ms Chalmer said.

"Come on four eyes," Brian Alexander said as he stood and gestured for Fenton and Andy to follow him.

"Ah, what exactly was it Ms Chalmer asked us to do? I think I missed a detail or two." Fenton thought he would feel Brian out about what they were supposed to do without letting him know he hadn't been paying attention.

"What's the matter Tug, get caught dozing off?" Brian wasn't particularly helpful. "We're supposed to get the new reading books from the book room in the basement. You aren't afraid to go down there are you Tug?" Brian winked and poked Andy with his elbow. "I've heard there are some pretty creepy things down there that reach out and..." Brian was getting into the description of what waited for them at the bottom of the stairs when Andy said, "Ease up will you Brian," and slowed as he approached the top of the stairs. "You're kidding about creepy things aren't you?" "Think about it Andy, would Principal Logan allow bad things to live in the basement with little kids around?" Brian paused and Andy relaxed a little. When he saw the look on Andy's face he couldn't resist adding, "I'd keep an eye out for bats hanging from the ceiling if I were you."

Having made their way down the stairs, they stopped in front of a door with a sign that said, *Grades 3-5 Reading Books*. They'd just opened the door and were about to step inside when they heard a **Whomp** and were shrouded in darkness as the lights in the school went out.

Fenton heard a familiar voice coming from the next room. "I am thinking a thought that an almost apprentice wish wizard approximately my height with no experience in matters of this nature should not have attempted to turn around in what I have discovered is a room of electrical things."

He heard the shuffling feet of the almost apprentice wish wizard in high top sneakers with no socks moving slowly down the darkened hallway. Instruments clanged as the backpack followed his waddling movements.

"What's that?" Andy asked and threw his arms in front of his face to ward off any bats that might have let go of the ceiling and taken flight when the lights went out.

"Yeah," Brian added, "this isn't funny. Not funny at all. Is this another one of your goof ups Fenton?"

Fenton started to answer but stopped when he heard a voice behind him whisper, "Numerous apologies are certainly in order Mr. Norman sir for the most terrible, something or other problem created by my two iron." Fenton guessed he was talking about the golf club in his backpack. "It, through no fault of it's own or mine for that matter, while turning around, came in contact with a knob thing in the room called electrical. Perhaps, Mr. Norman," Fenton heard Sheldon mumble as he rummaged in his backpack, "would allow me to provide a device which I have, while speaking to you, found and removed from my Almost Apprentice Kit Level 1."

Fenton felt something slip into his hand, discovered it was a flashlight, and feeling along the top, found the button that turned it on.

The hallway in front of the book room filled with light.

He heard the confusion upstairs as frightened children tried to find their way through the darkened hallways. Someone on the loud speaker was calling for Mr. Blaine the custodian, who usually took a nap in the boiler room this time in the afternoon.

The younger students were crying and their teachers encouraged them to hold the hand of the child next to them

The boys, aided by the flashlight in Fenton's hand, huddled in the middle of the basement hallway.

"Let's get out of here while we have a chance," Brian wailed, "this place gives me the creeps."

Andy nodded, too frightened to talk.

"Hey doofus," Brian called to Fenton who was walking away from them. "Where do you think your going?" Then, realizing the only source of light was moving away from him hollered, "Wait up Fenton, I was kidding about the doofus thing." He grabbed Andy's arm and hurried after Fenton.

Something Sheldon said about the two iron making contact with a knob got Fenton's attention. The beam of the flashlight moved across the floor and came to rest at the bottom of a door. The light moved up and stopped at the words, **Electrical Room**.

Fenton opened the door.

On the far wall was a gray box. He remembered seeing one like it at his house only it was a lot smaller. He'd gone downstairs with his father one night when the lights went out and he showed him how to reset the circuit breaker.

He pushed a mop bucket out of the way and stepped closer to the box.

"Be careful Fenton," Brian warned, "it could explode or something."

Andy nodded he agreed with Brian.

Both boys stayed close to Fenton as he moved toward the box.

"I'll hold the light," Fenton told Brian in a calm, steady voice, "while you read the instructions on the box."

Brian leaned forward and squinted. "I can't make it out," he said and shook his head as he backed away. "The printing's too small."

"Andy, see if you can do any better." Fenton's arm was getting tired from holding the flashlight over his head.

Andy tilted his head to one side and said, "I can read the big word *IMPORTANT* but that's about it. Sorry."

Fenton looked at the sign and wondered what was wrong with these guys, the printing was clear as a bell. "If power is lost," he read out loud with no difficulty at all, "push the button." A red arrow pointed to a blue button.

Fenton pushed the button, heard another **Whomp**, and was relieved when the light in the electrical room, as well as those in the rest of the building, came on.

He heard the excited voices of children as they turned around and hurried back to their classrooms.

"Maybe those glasses do some good after all," Brian said as he and Andy dashed out of the electrical room and down the hall, hoping to reach the stairs before the lights went out again.

Fenton saw the toes of a pair of high top sneakers sticking into the hallway from the entrance to the book room.

"Sheldon?" Fenton whispered.

He heard the sound of the equipment in his backpack clang as the door opened and Sheldon stepped out.

"I'm sorry about the, ah, you know, thing about my name. I was...I don't know." Fenton struggled to find a way to apologize.

"If I may call you Fenton at this moment sir, the words coming from your mouth, said Norman but, and I apologize for looking at personal items such as your lunch box without your permission but even someone of approximately my height could see *Fenton* written on the handle."

Fenton blushed, ashamed he'd tried to deceive someone as innocent as Sheldon.

"Well Mr. Fenton sir you are, if I might say with some pride and I believe heartfelt enthusiasm, a hero in that you and your thumb of course, brought light back to the Buffalo school. Now," Sheldon rummaged through his backpack and produced a sheet of paper with, **Almost Apprentice Level 1 Evaluation Form** printed across the top, "if you would at some point in say this moment or the next, answer the question printed here." He pointed to a place on the evaluation form.

Fenton read the first line. *In my opinion, Sheldon, equipped with a used Almost Apprentice Kit Level 1 purchased at the price of $29.95, discharged his duty; less than one might expect from an almost apprentice wish wizard.*

What one might expect from an almost apprentice wish wizard...

So well I get choked up thinking about it.

He saw a large box outlined in black with an explanation beneath it that said to place the appropriate number in the box. *"Do not,"* it said, *"let any part of the number extend outside the box because this form will be graded by someone who doesn't understand why people are so careless they can't write a number inside a box."*

Fenton took the blue crayon Sheldon handed him and carefully wrote three inside the box.

A smile replaced the worried look on Sheldon's face. "I am profuse in my thanks for such an upwardly noble number sir. Profuse is all anyone in my position could possibly..." He broke into tears and hugged Fenton's knees.

He took the evaluation form from Fenton, folded it in half, and waddled down the hallway. He stopped, unfolded the paper, looked at it again, and muttered, "The Fenton lad gave me a three and no part of the number extends beyond the box. How profuse of him."

Fenton entered the book room and gathered an armload of *Adventures in Reading for the Third Grade Student.* He turned off the light switch with his elbow and pushed the door closed with his foot.

He looked up when reached the bottom of the stairs and saw Principal Logan and several teachers huddled around Brian and Andy. As usual, Brian was doing the talking. "... and of course when the lights went out I knew exactly what to do since I recently checked out, *Thomas Edison, Boy Electrician* from the school library. If you will allow me to say so Mrs. Shoemaker, you have assembled an impressive collection of technical books."

Mrs. Shoemaker looked puzzled. She couldn't remember seeing Brian near the library, much less in it.

Brian looked away as Fenton climbed the stairs with an armload of books. When he reached the first floor, Fenton used the top book to push his glasses in place.

When Brian was sure Fenton was far enough away, he turned back to his group of admirers. "So I said to my buddy Andy, if we're going to save the children upstairs we better get to the electrical room on the double."

Fenton heard Principal Logan ask Brian something and listened as he answered, "Seriously? Me, afraid of the dark? You've got to be kidding."

Fenton placed the books on top of Ms Chalmer's desk and returned to his seat. He noticed a piece of paper sticking from beneath the top of his desk.

He looked around and discovered the room was empty. Once Ms Chalmer got the class outside because of the lights going out, she decided they should take an early recess.

He removed the piece of paper and unfolded it. *"wISh PErSon eVOLutioN fROm,"* was printed clumsily across the top.

A number three, drawn with a purple crayon, filled the entire page.

Fenton ran to the window and looked out in time to see part of a rake slip behind the picnic table. The instrument for measuring wind speed was spinning.

Fenton glanced at the evaluation form and said, "He gave me a three. How profuse of him."

When he looked again the almost apprentice wish wizard was gone.

Chapter 5
BeWilbered

Fenton Alowishus Tug pressed his head against the back of the seat in front of him and wondered if Mr. Fleener had decided to take the long way to his stop, he felt he'd been riding for hours.

It fits, he told himself, the way my day has gone.

First there was the missed fly ball during morning recess. He'd taken his position in right field and Derrick Pilcher was up. He'd never kicked the ball out of the infield Fenton took his eyes off the game for a second to watch the girls jump rope and **WHAM** the ball hit him in the head. He found his glasses and put them on in time to hear the guys on the other team laughing as Derrick, waving to the crowd, crossed home plate.

Then there was the tray incident in the cafeteria. While waiting in line to pay for his lunch Buddy Donnell said, "Think fast," and threw what turned out to be an empty milk carton toward him. Buddy had poured the milk in his glass, sealed the carton back up, and acted like it was full when he threw it. Fenton had tightened his grip on the tray and lifted up, hoping to balance the weight of the milk carton against the food on his plate. When it landed he pushed up with enough force to catch a full carton but too much for an empty one and flipped the chicken nuggets and Jell-O Surprise on his tray, over his shoulder and onto Regina Filbine's notebook.

"Smart move Fenton," she said as she looked for a place to dump the food. "Real smart."

In the afternoon he'd been thinking about something else when Ms Chalmer asked him to work a problem at the chalkboard. He hadn't noticed Brian Alexander had tied his shoe laces together. He stood, took a step toward the board, and fell between the row of chairs. He wondered if he'd ever forget looking up and seeing everyone pointing and laughing at him.

Finally there was the note from Irene Stubbs that said Gloria Bishop thought he was cute. He hadn't noticed the *NOT!* written on the back . He'd gone to the pencil sharpener near Gloria's desk and smiled his best smile, the one he practiced in front of the bathroom mirror when there's nothing to watch on TV.

When he finished sharpening his pencil he turned around in time to see Gloria act like she was gagging and Irene trying hard not to laugh.

And now Brian Alexander and Andy, sitting in the seat behind him, were replaying the scene in Ms Chalmer's room for the kids who'd missed it. "First he was up," Brian said. "Then he was down," Andy finished for him. They laughed so hard they had to lean against each other to keep from falling off the seat.

When the bus reached his stop, Fenton stood, turned around and told Brian, **"I wish you'd leave me alone."** Everyone was surprised, they'd never seen him like this. He was the kid who sat there and took it while Brian Alexander piled on the abuse. He struggled to find something really clever to say that would make Brian feel bad for the way they'd treated him but, with everyone watching, he couldn't. So he repeated, **"I wish you'd..."** before storming off the bus.

As the bus pulled away he could see Brian and Andy punching each other and laughing while the other passengers stared out the windows and wondered, "*What's wrong with him?*"

When he walked through the kitchen his mother told him he forgot to feed his gold fish before leaving for school.

As he passed through the family room his brother Felix said, "If you're thinking about riding your bike forget it, both tires are flat."

He climbed the stairs, stopped in front of the door to his room, and wondered what the smell was. Had his mother painted his room while he was at school? Or shampooed the rug?

Then it came to him. There was no smell like the smell of airplane glue. He tried to remember the last time he'd built a model airplane and the answer was never, he'd started several but hadn't finished them.

When he opened the door, he saw a middle-aged man wearing glasses sitting at his desk. He was bent over, pushing straight pins into a corkboard. He squinted while he worked and his hair hung across his forehead. He absentmindedly pushed it back with his free hand, become absorbed in what he was doing, and not notice when it fell back where it had been.

He wore light blue coveralls and red high top sneakers. He'd turned the desk lamp so the light was shining on his work.

Fenton cleared his throat to get the visitor's attention.

No luck.

He coughed.

No response.

Finally he dropped his backpack on the floor and asked, "What are you doing in my room?"

At first he thought the person was ignoring him but he slowly sat up and blinked in surprise when he saw Fenton standing next to the desk. "School out already?" the visitor asked in a high pitched voice. There was a whistling sound when he spoke, like when you put a piece of grass between your thumbs and blow on it.

He turned so Fenton could get a better look at what he was working on and said, "Piper Cub."

"What?" Fenton was puzzled. He must not of heard him right, that can't be his name.

Seeing the look of confusion on Fenton's face the visitor pointed to the desk, "What I'm working on is called a Piper Cub." Seeing no sign of recognition from Fenton he added, "The airplane. A Piper Cub."

Fenton noticed when he pointed a piece of balsa wood was stuck to the tip of his finger. It was curved on top and a square notch had been cut out of both ends. Fenton recognized it as part of the wing of the airplane.

"Oh," Fenton said and laughed, "I thought it was your name." He expected the visitor to introduce himself but he didn't so he asked, "What is it? Your name?"

The visitor was lost in thought as he stared at his work. He seemed to be looking for a missing piece of the wing. Fenton started to repeat the question but before he could, the visitor mumbled, "You were, ah," as his eyes moved from the model to Fenton. "Wilber. The name's Wilber."

As he talked he searched through his pockets, looking for something. He relaxed when he found it and handed Fenton his business card. Or, tried to since it was stuck to his finger. When Fenton pulled the card loose, he noticed a white piece of paper stuck to Wilber's thumb.

Fenton looked at the card and saw the name *Wilber.* Then there was a hole where his last name had been, and below that, *Flight Instructor, Wish Wizards, Inc.*

While Fenton read the card, Wilber leaned forward and tugged on the pins holding the airplane wing in place to see if the glue was dry. He didn't seem to notice the piece of paper stuck to his thumb.

"That's great," Fenton shook his head to emphasize his disappointment. "I'm having the worst day of my life and they send a flight instructor?"

Wilber took the card from Fenton, read it, mumbled, "That says it all," and tucked the card in a pocket of his coveralls. "You said something about a bad day?" Wilber said as he tapped the wing with his finger. "Or your worst day? Something about your day."

Fenton wondered how anyone who needed glasses with lenses as thick as Wilber's was allowed to fly an airplane.

Like he was reading Fenton's mind Wilber said, "Anyone can fly an airplane, it's the landing and taking off that's tricky."

"Isn't that considered flying?" Fenton was confused when Wilber broke flying into three parts.

"Not really. They're totally different activities; taking off, flying, and landing. And the important thing is, you've got to do them in that order." Wilber rubbed his chin trying to find a way to explain such a complicated idea to an inquisitive third grader.

He decided to try a different approach. "Let's say, and I'm just making this up as I go along so don't press me for details. But let's say someone is riding home on a school bus and the kids in the seat behind him are talking about a *particular* incident that happened in a *particular* classroom involving the shoestrings of a *particular* person. And let's say that *particular* person stood up, said something he shouldn't have because he was angry, and *that same person* stomped off the bus."

"I didn't stomp off..." Fenton stopped when Wilber held up his hand.

"I said I'm making this up, I didn't say the *particular* person was you." It took a moment for Wilber to remember where he was going with his example. "Okay, got it." he mumbled, pleased he was able to recall where he was before Fenton interrupted. "It wouldn't make sense if the person stomped off the bus then yelled at the passengers would it? The kids on the bus wouldn't know why he was upset. People driving by would see a kid standing on the sidewalk yelling at a school bus and think he was saying goodbye to his friends. And a woman walking her dog might think he was talking to her."

This whole line of thinking didn't make sense to Fenton. Of course you have to take off before you land. That was obvious. But how did that tie in to a kid yelling at a bus?

"All I'm saying is there's an order to things and some people, no matter how hard they try, never figure it out." Fenton looked confused so Wilber decided to try a different approach. He stuck his hands in his pockets, walked to the door, came back and said, "It's like making a snowball before it snows." He looked at Fenton hoping that cleared things up.

"That's so obvious," Fenton was still thinking about the incident on the bus and almost missed the snowball example. "What good would it do to wait until your off the bus to let people know you're upset? Anybody can see that."

"Anybody?" Wilber said as he returned to Fenton's desk and started removing the pins that held the airplane wing in place.

"How could you possibly..." Fenton was having trouble keeping up with Wilber's examples.

"Take popcorn." Wilber cut off the question Fenton was about to ask when he thought of something else.

"Huh?" Was all Fenton could say. He wondered how Wilber could jump from making snowballs before it snows to popcorn?

"First you pop the corn, then you eat it." Wilber said the words slowly, like the subject was so complicated he had to say it that way or Fenton wouldn't understand. "Not. The. Other. Way. Around. That's all I'm saying."

He looked at the ceiling for a moment then turned back to Fenton. "Okay, try this on for size. You can't eat an ice cream cone before you make the ice cream." There was a sound in his voice that suggested if Fenton didn't get it this time he didn't know what he'd do because he'd run out of examples.

"I understand what you're saying. I got it the first time." Fenton hated it when people thought he was too dumb to figure things out. "You could have left out the snowball and popcorn examples." Fenton stopped to take a breath. "What does that have to do with being made fun of, getting mad, and leaving the bus?"

Wilber shook his head and said slowly, "First you take off. First it snows. And first you pop corn."

Fenton put his hands on his hips, stuck out his chin and said, "So?"

Wilber got a pained expression on his face like he didn't want to do what he was about to do but was forced to because he'd run out of ideas. He reached under Fenton's desk and pulled a movie projector from a worn, canvas bag. Fenton noticed it was the same kind they use at his school.

Wilber pushed the switch and the movie started.

On the wall above his bed, Fenton saw the same scratchy white blocks that appear when Ms Chalmer showed movies in her room. He saw an airplane landing, more white blocks, then the school playground. He looked closer and saw himself jogging to right field.

"That's me," he said in surprise as he saw himself turn toward the infield, pick up some grass and throw it in the air, checking to see if there was a breeze that might effect the flight of the ball. He saw his lips move and knew he was going through his pre-pitch chatter, *"We got no kicker at the plate, no kicker Leennnyyy,"* he remembered hollering to the pitcher Lenny Gilstrap.

He leaned forward in his chair when he saw Derrick Pilcher step to the plate.

"That's today," he gasped. "How did you, I mean, **that's today**."

Rather than answer, Wilber pointed to the wall. Fenton looked back in time to see himself straighten up, put a hand against his forehead, shielding his eyes from the sun and look around. He remembered hearing the drone of an airplane overhead then turned back to the game ready to play.

"Here," he heard Wilber say, and turned a knob on the projector that slowed things down to half speed.

Fenton saw his head turn and look at the girls jumping rope as Lenny rolled the ball to Derrick. He saw Derrick bunt the ball and dash to first base.

He saw himself watching the girls jump rope

He saw Darrin Boswell kick a fly ball to Billy Gilsky in left field.

He saw himself watching the girls jump rope.

He saw Brian Alexander kick a ball to the first baseman advancing Derrick to second.

He saw himself watching the girls jump rope.

He saw Marcus Gage loop one over the head of Simon Trimble for a single and Derrick run to third.

He saw himself watching the girls jump rope.

He saw Rudy "Big Foot" Griggs step to the plate. They call him Big Foot because he can kick the ball anywhere he wants with the power of someone twice his age. He saw Rudy look to right field and smile as he recognized Fenton's attention was not on the game.

Impossible, Fenton thought.

He saw the ball explode off Rudy's foot and sail straight for his head.

He saw an airplane take off, then the space above his bed went blank.

"That can't be, I just looked away for a second," he mumbled even though the film showed otherwise.

Wilber started the projector again.

"That's Ms Chalmer's room?" Fenton said in surprise.

The film looked like it had been shot by someone standing outside the classroom.

He saw an airplane landing then saw himself, turned sideways in his chair, staring out the window. The camera swung around and showed Ms Chalmer writing something on the chalkboard. It swung back and he was looking out of the window. It swung down and showed Brian Alexander sneaking up the aisle to tie his shoestrings together.

"I get it," Fenton groaned, "I don't need to see anymore."

On the wall an airplane landed.

Wilber turned off the movie projector and stuck it back in the canvas bag.

"What's the point?" Fenton was embarrassed at being caught daydreaming. He was sure if the movie had continued, it would show he was the victim of his own carelessness.

"There's an order to things," Wilber said softly. "Learn the order and prevent disaster."

"I guess I tried to land before I took off," Fenton volunteered as he moved to the window in his room, looked out, and thought about what he'd seen.

When he turned to ask Wilber to tell him more about the order of things, he discovered he was gone. The only thing suggesting he'd been there was the faint smell of airplane glue and a piece of a business card stuck to the edge of his desk.

Things at school were going better for Fenton the next day. There'd been no major calamities in the class room before recess. When his team ran on the field for the morning kickball game Fenton took his place in right field. He went through his routine, tossing grass in the air to check the direction of the wind and pulling his cap down so it wouldn't fall off if he had to chase a fly ball.

As the first kicker strolled confidently to home plate Fenton's attention was pulled away from the game by shrieks of laughter from the girls side of the playground. He started to look their way but stopped when he noticed a preschool kid in light blue coveralls and red high top sneakers crouched down, turning the propeller of a model airplane.

First you take off, Fenton reminded himself, *then you land. Not the other way around.*

He smiled, turned back to the game and hollered toward the infield, *"Hey, hey kicker.* "We got no kicker at the plate. *No kicker Leennnyyy."*

Chapter 6
Kick It Here

Fenton Alowishus Tug was worried.

His mother told him, "Just do you're best dear."

His father lowered his cup of coffee and said, "Give it the old college try son."

His older brother shook his head and said solemnly, "Coach Barnett is going to make you wish you'd never heard the word kickball." When he finished he chuckled and asked his father to pass the mashed potatoes.

Fenton excused himself from the table.

It was Friday night and starting Monday, for five days in a row, Coach Peewee Barnett was holding his annual kickball camp. On the final day, the legendary coach of the Golden Buffaloes picked the top fifteen players to represent Buffalo Bill Cody Elementary School for the fall kickball season.

Fenton slowly climbed the stairs to his room. When he reached the top step he turned around and sat down. He closed his eyes and whispered, "I wish my parents hadn't signed me up for kickball camp."

He listened but heard…nothing.

No clearing of a throat.

No belch or wheeze.

No klunk from a wish wizard's bag hitting the floor or the pop of a wand.

All he heard was the gurgle of the pump in the fish tank.

He opened the door to his room and saw no one large or small leaning against the wall or sitting at his desk.

"I guess I'm on my own," he mumbled as he pulled back the covers and fell on his bed.

After breakfast the next morning his father asked if he wanted to run a few errands with him.

Fenton considered his options. Would it be better to sit around, worry about kickball camp and watch cartoons he'd seen a dozen times, or drive around and make a million stops at stores that had nothing interesting for kids his age.

He shrugged and said, "Sure. Why not?"

Their first stop was at *Handyman's Hardware* where his father after looking at every paint brush in the store, finally bought one. Fenton decided to stay in the car when they got to the dry cleaners.

While he waited he played his usual time killing game; closing his eyes and trying to remember the names of the shops on his side of the street. When he finished he'd do the same with those on the other side.

He went through the list, then opened his eyes and started with the shop on the corner to see how many he got right.

He stopped when he reached the middle of the block. Something was wrong. A new store occupied the place where *Dinglemans Auto Insurance* had been.

He started over, going through the list and thinking he'd made a mistake. Maybe Dinglemens was on a different street. He could picture the cartoon character on the window standing by a cartoon automobile with a bashed in front fender and Band-Aid over the headlight. Beneath the cartoon was their slogan, *Before the dent, call Ding.*

In its place, where Dinglemans had been for as long as he could remember, was a store called **KICK IT HERE**. He had to squint to read the words on the large kickball painted on the window. He couldn't believe his eyes when, beneath the ball, in white letters, he saw *The Ultimate Store for the Kickball Enthusiast.*

He had to check it out.

He found his father standing in line at the dry cleaners and said he'd be back in a minute, he was going to a store in the middle of the block.

"Make it snappy," his father told him, upset they couldn't find the pants to his new gray suit.

Fenton walked down the sidewalk and stopped in front of **KICK IT HERE**. He put his hands against the plate glass window, pressed his forehead against his hands, and looked inside.

There were no products on the shelves because there were no shelves. No kick balls, shoes, or other equipment were on display. No posters of famous kickball players covered the walls and there was no counter where you'd expect to see a cash register.

The only thing he saw was a middle-aged woman wearing green sweatpants, white sneakers, and a *Kick It Here* tee shirt running a vacuum cleaner over the beige carpet.

"That explains it," Fenton mumbled as he stepped away from the window, "they're not open yet."

He turned to leave but stopped when he saw a sign that said, **Yes Were Open** swinging from the door handle like someone had just put it there.

Fenton opened the door and stepped inside.

The woman turned off the vacuum cleaner, looked at Fenton and said, "Welcome to *Kick It Here*. Can I show you something in our line of kickball equipment?"

Fenton looked around and confirmed what he'd seen from outside, the store was completely empty. "Ahh. I...," was all he could say.

She spoke a little louder. "Is there something...," she stopped when she saw the confused look on his face. "I get it," she said and nodded knowingly as she followed his gaze around the empty room. "You're used to seeing hangers with clothes and shelves stacked with equipment. When you don't see them, you automatically assume we're not open for business. Am I right?"

"Well, I mean sure, who wouldn't?" the answer seemed to her question seemed obvious to him.

"Try me," the salesperson challenged.

"I'm sorry?" Fenton said.

"You think I'm giving you the run around," she said as she leaned forward and bounced on her toes like a tennis player waiting for a serve. "So, try me."

"Okay," Fenton said slowly, stalling for time while he thought of what to ask for. "I want a *Professional Kickball* made by the *Stonum Company* and signed by *Quantos*, without a doubt the greatest kickball player in the world."

The salesperson walked confidently to a door Fenton guessed led to a storeroom. That explains it he thought and pictured a room crammed with everything from shin guards to the latest kickball shoes.

She opened the door and yelled "*Stonum kb with Quantos sig.*"

She looked at Fenton and smiled.

He heard a voice from the back room mumble something but couldn't make out what it was.

The salesperson frowned, closed the door, walked over and said, "Sorry, we don't have a *Professional Kickball* made by *Stonum* and signed by *Quantos*."

"How about a *Professional Kickball* without the signature?" Fenton asked.

She went to the door, pushed it open, and hollered, "*Stonum kb hold the sig.*"

Fenton heard the voice and like the first time couldn't understand what he said. Or she, he reminded himself, it could be a woman with a deep voice.

She shook her head. "Sorry. No *Professional Kickball* with or without a signature."

"I'll make this easy for you," Fenton could feel himself getting angry. So far he'd made two requests and she'd failed at both of them. "A kickball. Any make. No signature."

From the way she walked to the door to the storeroom you couldn't tell she'd experienced two failures. Watching her stride confidently across the showroom floor you would have thought she'd kicked a home run with the bases loaded.

"*Kb,*" she called to the person in back.

She tapped her foot while she waited.

Fenton heard what sounded like someone tripping over a box or falling off a ladder. The sound was followed by a muffled cry like whoever was back there had stubbed his toe or bumped his head.

The salesperson raised her shoulders and lifted her hands. "We're out of kick balls. We've got nothing. Nada. Zilch."

"**WHAT KIND OF PLACE IS THIS?**" Fenton asked angrily. He felt like a doofus believing someone could produce something from an empty showroom. "**IS THERE ANYTHING BACK THERE?**"

The salesperson ignored the tone of his voice, opened the door and hollered, *"Potluck."*

After waiting what seemed to Fenton like forever, he heard something slide down a ramp, sail out of an opening in the wall, and land on the carpeted floor.

She picked it up, crossed the empty room, handed it to Fenton and said, "There you go."

"What is it?" he asked as he turned it over in his hand.

"A complimentary key ring," she said like she couldn't figure out why anyone would want anything else. She tapped it and said proudly, "It's made of stainless steel. You can't bend it, you can't break it, and it won't rust." She paused, pointed at the key ring, and told him to turn it over.

He did and saw **Kick It Here** stamped in the metal, the tops of the letters rising above the surface.

He couldn't believe it. In the entire place, show room and storeroom, the only thing they could come up with was a key ring? It's useless, he thought. "It's useless," he said, "I don't have a key."

"No problem," she said as she removed a key from a ring hooked to her belt and slipped it on Fenton's.

"What's it open?" Fenton asked. "What's it unlock?"

"I have no idea," the salesperson answered. "A car door? Possibly a locker?" She looked away deep in thought then turned back to him. "The important thing is, you have a key for your key ring," she said as she handed it back to Fenton, "and we have a satisfied customer."

"That does it," Fenton said, "I'm out of here." He stuck the key ring in his pocket and stomped out of the store. He glanced back and watched the salesperson unplug the vacuum cleaner and roll up the cord.

Then it hit him. A store with no products. The odd looking salesperson. The unseen worker in back who mumbled when he talked and couldn't find anything, if in fact there was anything to find. He pulled the key ring from his pocket and noticed for the first time, at the end of *Kick It Here*, a circle formed by the letters, *Wish Wizards Inc.*. He couldn't see the wishbone of a turkey in the center of the circle but was sure it was there.

"She's a wish wizard!" Fenton said loud enough for several walking by to wonder if he was talking to them. He didn't care what they thought, this was great news, they hadn't ignored him after all.

He spun around with the intention of going back inside, letting her know he'd figured out what was going on and finding out what advice she could give about surviving kickball camp. He found the door was locked and a, *Sorry, We're Closed* sign swinging from the handle like someone had just put it there.

His dad was hanging his suit on a hook over the back window when Fenton walked up. "Well?" His father asked.

"Nothing," Fenton said as he pulled the seat belt over his shoulder and stuck it in the clasp.

His father backed out of the parking place, made a U-turn, and headed for the *Brenda's Bountiful Bakery* to pick up cinnamon rolls for their Sunday breakfast.

Fenton glanced out the car window as they drove by *Kick It Here*. He sat up and took a closer look at the store window. The cartoon figure was back, and beneath the wrecked cartoon car he saw, **"Before the dent call Ding."**

He slid down in his seat, put his hands on his head, and wondered what was going on.

He hated to admit it but his brother was right. After the first day of camp he wished he'd never heard the word kickball. If they weren't doing wind sprints or running the obstacle course, Coach Barnett had them doing push-ups and jumping jacks.

Worse than being out of breath, bruised from climbing ropes, or walking across wooden beams, was the constant presence of Coach Barnett. Fenton felt he was the only player on the field because all he heard was, "Come on Tug, keep up with those guys." Or, "Are you trying to give my camp a bad name? Could you just once, make it through the obstacle course without falling off something?"

Later in the morning the coach crouched next to him. "Congratulations, you're the first guy on the team to let your feet hit the deck." They'd been lying on their backs with their legs stretched out and their feet hovering inches above the ground. Fenton shook from exertion but it was no use, his feet touched the field and it was over.

"Gentlemen," Coach Barnett stood and called to the team. The other kids lowered their feet, sat up, and faced him. "Mister Tug," Coach Barnett said as he grabbed the back of Fenton's tee shirt and pulled him up so he had to stand on his toes to keep from losing his balance, "lasted a grand total of three seconds in the leg lift." A few of the guys snickered but Coach Barnett silenced them with a look and asked, "You know what that means don't you?"

One of them shouted, "He's a wimp."

Coach Barnett waved his hand, letting them know he wasn't expecting an answer.

It became quiet as everyone waited to hear what terrible thing Fenton would have to do. Pitch kicking practice all week? Take the equipment to the gym when practice was over?

Fenton heard a bus in the school parking lot close its doors and start up. He wished he was on it, he didn't care where it was going. "What it means is," Coach Barnett interrupted his thoughts, "Mister Tug is going to join me on the bleachers."

"Huh," Fenton heard several say. Someone asked the kid next to him if he thought the Coach was serious or just joking around?

"Yes sir," Coach Barnett continued, unfazed by their groans and sarcastic comments. "We'll be sitting on the top row, having a cool drink of water and watching the rest of you run a lap around the field for every second Mr. Tug's feet were off the ground." Fenton heard a few players groan and several gave him a dirty look.

Coach Barnett asked Fenton. "How many seconds was that Mr. Tug?"

"Three sir," Fenton mumbled and looked at the top of his shoes.

"I'm a little hard of hearing Fenton so I missed what you said,. Could you speak a little louder?" After he said it, Coach Barnett leaned toward him and put a hand to his ear in an exaggerated way that drew laughter from the players.

"Three sir!" Fenton said as loud as he could.

"If my math is correct," Coach Barnett said addressing the other players, "that boils down to three laps for each member of the team." No one moved because they thought he was joking. All doubt ended when he hollered, **"Move it!"**

As the team got to their feet and started jogging toward first base, Coach Barnett turned Fenton around, pointed to the bleachers and said, "Let me show you to your seat Mr. Tug."

Things stayed that way for three more days. Whether it was push-ups or deep knee bends, Fenton couldn't keep up with the older boys. Most of his day was spent doing what Coach Barnett called *QBT, quality bench time.* That meant he sat in the bleachers while those trying to make the team perfected their kickball skills.

Sometime during the week he lost the **Kick It Here** key ring. He figured it was useless to look for it, he'd been all over the field. He'd checked under the bleachers thinking it had fallen out of his pocket while sitting with Coach Barnett but, after looking through crushed plastic cups and wadded up hot dog wrappers and not finding it, he'd given up.

He saw his chance of making the team mingle with the clouds of dust churned up by runners as the circled the bases.

To add insult to injury, in the middle of the week Coach Barnett placed an umbrella over his seat and announced to the team, "We don't want Mr. Tug to get a sunburn do we?"

He thought of quitting.

As the camp progressed several players were injured. One kid sprained his ankle, and another got a badly scraped knee sliding into second base. A player who was on last years team dislocated his shoulder and was lost for the season when he ran into the left field fence while chasing a fly ball.

On the last day of camp Coach Barnett selected the fifteen players for this year's team. The way it stood, twenty candidates remained on the roster and Fenton was one of them.

Late in the afternoon they were doing a drill called *GC* and stood for *Game Conditions.* Players who'd made the team were in the field and one by one those in the dugout took their chance at getting on base.

"All you have to do is make it to first against the best defensive kickball team in the city," Coach Barnett said as he paced in front of the dugout and gestured toward the players on the field before finishing with, "and you're on the team."

One by one the kickers ground or flew out. One kid, finding the pressure to make the team more than he could handle, kicked early and completely missed the ball.

Occasionally Coach Barnett blew his whistle and the infield would move in a foot or two expecting a bunt. Or the first baseman would charge down the foul line toward the kicker and the rest of the infield shifted over to cover his position.

Coach is right, Fenton thought, they're definitely good.

When it was his turn to kick he heard the outfielders shout:

"Fenton Tug
is an odd little creature,
tried to make the team
by sitting in the bleachers."

The rest of the players laughed and threw their caps in the air.

Tweet. Coach Barnett blew his whistle and hollered, "Settle down boys. Tug's the last kicker. Get him out and this year's camp is over." The boys cheered at a chance to end practice early, then grew serious and settled into their positions.

While Fenton stood at home plate waiting for the pitcher to ask him how he wanted the ball, something in right field caught his eye. The sun was reflecting off an object near Brian Alexander's foot.

Fenton remembered what the Wish Wizard said about the key ring. "You can't bend it, you can't break it, and it won't rust." Then he thought of the name of the store stamped on the front, **Kick It Here.** Why not, he thought, I've got nothing to lose. He hollered, "Slow and bouncy," to the pitcher, the perfect call for the kick he wanted to make.

As soon as the pitcher released the ball, **Tweet, tweet,** came from Coach Barnett's whistle and the third baseman started down the foul line toward home plate. The moment he left his position, the outfielders shifted to cover the left side of the field.

Fenton turned to the right and the pitcher laughed, thinking he was afraid of getting run over by the hard charging third baseman.

The ball rolled toward him and **boom**, it flew off his foot headed straight for the spot Brian Alexander occupied before the shift. Brian saw what was happening and tried to change direction but his feet slid out from under him and he went down.

The entire team watched in disbelief as the ball bounced through the outfield, eventually coming to rest under the picnic table at the far end of the field.

Fenton wiped his eyes with the sleeve of his shirt as he rounded the bases; he didn't want the guys on the team to see he was so happy he was crying.

He jumped the last few feet and landed on home plate.

None of the fielders moved, they didn't know what to do; no one had kicked a home run on them before.

The **tweet,** from Coach Barnett's whistle was followed by, "Well don't just stand there like a bunch of ninnies, get the ball." He turned to Fenton and said, "Nice kick Tug, get your jersey from the box by the bleachers. You made the team."

"Just a second Coach," Fenton said as he started towards right field, "I've got to look…" As he ran to the outfield he pointed to the spot where he'd seen the key ring. He found it, picked it up, and started back when he saw the salesperson from *Kick It Here* standing by first base.

"Super kick Fenton," she said as he jogged toward her. "Reminds me a lot of the one Quantos made in the '93 Kickball World Series."

"You saw Quantos play?" Fenton couldn't believe he was talking to an eye witness to the greatest kickball player in the world.

"I did, but don't let me hold you up," the salesperson tilted her head toward the box of jerseys. "If it isn't too much trouble, could I have the key I gave you? I kind of need it."

"Sure," Fenton said as he worked the key off the ring and handed it to her. "Did you find out what it's for?"

The *Kick It Here* salesperson nodded and blushed. "It opens the door to Flounder Tower and Ken Flounder is furious because no one can get in until I unlock it."

Chapter 7
AWAY GAME
Part 1: The Eindorf Connection

Fenton Alowishus Tug couldn't believe he could be so stupid. He felt like the kid in the comic strip where the girl tells him she'll hold the football while he kicks it then, at the last second, pulls it away and he yells, "ARRUGHH," as he's falling.
He wondered how he could be such a doofus.

When Coach Peewee Barnett called his home and talked to his parents, Fenton couldn't wait for them to get off the phone and find out what was going on. When they finally did, he discovered Bobby Eindorf, owner of Eindorf's Quality Trucks & Cars, *If Its Got A Wheel, We've Got A Deal*, heard about the fall kickball games being canceled because of repairs to the school playground. He'd volunteered to pay for the team to go to the Mid-America Kickball Championships the following weekend. Peewee Barnett had been his coach when he attended Buffalo Bill Cody Elementary and he wanted to do something for the team to make up for the loss of their season. The tournament was in Willisburg, a town 200 miles north of Stemsville, Fenton's hometown. They'd ride to the tournament in his bus, stay overnight in a motel, and return Sunday evening after the championship game.

"Folks," Coach Barnett explained at the parents meeting a few days before the tournament, "this aint going to be no joy ride. During my coaching career I've spent my share of bus time but I'll honest with you, if we don't bring home the first place trophy, that's all it's gonna be for me, just another long bus ride."

The day before the trip, the players gathered around Coach Barnett for instructions. Instead of having them stretch or run wind sprints like he usually did, he looked at his watch and scanned the street like he was expecting someone. He'd tell a story about a team he'd coached then go through the same routine; look at his watch, check the street, and tell a story.

After standing around for twenty minutes, Fenton saw a bus turn the corner and pull into the school parking lot. A banner hung from the side with a picture of "Smiling" Bobby Eindorf on it.

Bobby had just finished an unsuccessful bid to become mayor of Stemsville and hadn't bothered to take the sign down. He'd actually been leading in many of the early polls. Printed across the bottom of the banner was his campaign slogan, *Hometown Boy, Hometown Ideas.*

Halfway through the race, the editor of the local newspaper *Under The Stemsville Clock,* received an anonymous call claiming it was Bobby Eindorf who, twenty years earlier, filled the Founders of Stemsville Memorial Fountain on the town square with soap. Bubbles flowed over the side and left a dark stain on the tiled walk around it. Soap had entered the pump that threw water high in the air causing it to overheat and shutdown. When the city council learned it would coast $2000 to repair the fountain, they voted to offer a $125 reward to anyone with information about the incident.

No one had come forward.

The caller claimed he had a photograph of Bobby, standing in front of the fountain, holding a box of soap. He hadn't said anything at the time because they played on the school kickball team but recently he'd bought a used car at Eindorf's that turned out to be a lemon and in the words of the caller, "What goes around, comes around."

After the disclosure Lester Middleton, the current Mayor, stood on the speakers platform holding a copy of the newspaper describing the incident and asked, "Are these the kind of *hometown ideas* Bobby's talking about? What can we expect next? Exploding golf balls? Water balloons thrown from the second floor of city hall? Do you really want a practical joker making decisions that will effect the future of our community?"

He put the paper down, propped an elbow on the podium and said in a way that sounded like one neighbor talking to another, "I hear if he loses he's going to TP the court house."

The paper called it "Fountaingate" and said the only chance Bobby had of winning was to close his eyes, toss a penny in the restored fountain, and make a wish.

Bobby received a total of sixteen votes; fourteen from the employees at Eindorf's Quality Trucks and Cars, one from his wife and his own. He also received a bill from the public works department for the cost of repairing the fountain.

The front door of the bus opened with a *whoosh* and Bobby Eindorf stepped out. He waved to the kids as he crossed the parking lot and gave Coach Barnett a hug. He gestured toward a spot in front of the team and said, "May I?"

"Be my guest," Coach Barnett stepped aside and let Bobby take his place in front of the players.

"Huddle up men," Bobby said and gestured for them to form a half circle in front of him.

He waited until everyone was quiet before saying, "Gentlemen, you may not be aware of it but playing kickball is a lot like selling cars." He took a moment to make eye contact with each boy. As he did they nodded like they knew what he was talking about. Fenton guessed it would be at least six years before any of them would be old enough to apply for a learners permit.

"First, to be successful in either endeavor you have to have a good manager." He reached out and placed a hand on Coach Barnett's shoulder. "And you've got, without a doubt, the best in the business. Let your coach know how much you appreciate him."

The boys cheered and hollered, "Way to go Coach," and, "You've got that right Bobby." They quickly corrected themselves and said, "We mean, Mr. Eindorf."

Bobby waved his hands to quiet them down. "But the best manager in the world can't do a thing unless he's backed up by a team of capable players." He paused for a moment then turned toward Coach Barnett. "I've watched your team practice when I could work it into my schedule and can say with confidence, you've got the best players in the city."

Some of the boys took off their caps and threw them in the air while others clapped and whistled.

Bobby waited for them to quiet down before saying, "**BUT,** even with a great coach and a team loaded with talent, you're only halfway there. You need one more thing to achieve greatness whether it's selling cars or winning kickball games."

"What is it Mr. Eindorf?" Concerned voices rose from the team. "What are we missing?"

"A car dealership like mine would fall flat as a pancake, indeed any dealership anywhere would go out of business just like that," he snapped his fingers causing several on the front row to jump, "if they don't have a star salesman. Someone they can count on to close the deal, complete the sale, and make the big play when the chips are down."

He pulled a handkerchief from the pocket of his plaid sport coat and dabbed at the corner of his eye. "You may find it hard to believe but twenty years ago, right after high school, I went to work at a local car dealership sweeping floors. But, because I played for Coach Barnett, I'd learned the value of hard work, dedication, and total commitment. The same qualities that made me a star athlete at Cody Elementary, helped me put away the broom and become the number one used car salesman in a three county area."

He paused and took a deep breath to help settle himself down. Thinking about his early years in the used car business had stirred old memories. Then, to everyone's surprise, he winked, broke into a smile and said, "Today I own the place."

The players shouted, "Hooray for Bobby Eindorf Used Trucks and Cars."

Fenton remembered watching him tell the same story on television with the same pauses and the same pulling of a handkerchief from the same sport coat pocket while giving a speech during the Mayor's race.

"I could go on about how I rose from a lowly floor sweeper to the owner of the most successful car dealership in the metropolitan area but I didn't come all the way over here to talk about me. No sir, I'm here to introduce your star salesman, you're new teammate, the one who'll make the big play when it's crunch time. One of my own flesh and blood."

Voices buzzed as each player shared with the one next to him what they knew about Misty Eindorf, Smiling Bobby's daughter. She's the same age they are but it was reported college scouts were already watching her and wondering what they had to do to get her to play for their team when she finished high school.

She's great at any sport she plays and is what many call, a natural athlete. "Gee whiz," the kids said to one another, "with Misty on our team we just wrapped up the championship." They patted each other on the back and showed a newfound confidence.

"Maybe when the other teams hear she's playing for us they'll turn around and go home," one of them suggested

While they were talking among themselves, Bobby Eindorf walked over to the door of the bus and said, "Boys let me introduce my son…"

"Son?" Several said at the same time. "Did he make a mistake and say son instead of daughter?" they wondered. "Don't tell us he's talking about…"

"Milton," Bobby said proudly as the door to the bus opened and he pointed to his son, standing on the top step.

"Not Milton Eindorf," the players moaned. "Not Milton the klutz. Milton the dork. Milton the geek. Milton the…" With the addition of Milton to the team they saw the championship trophy slip through their fingers and into the hands of their opponents.

Milton waved with his hand held close to his hip. "Hi guys," he said as he pushed his glasses a little higher on his nose. He started down the steps, lost his balance, and lurched forward. In an act of desperation, he grabbed the banner on the side of the bus. It ripped and split in two. Milton clung to the sign and swung back and forth, several feet above the ground.

Over his head, the part of the sign he was clinging to, said *Hometown Boy.*

His father walked over and helped him down.

Milton was wearing the tee shirt they'd all wear when they played in the tournament. It was navy blue and had the outline of a truck printed in white on the front. Beneath the truck was the saying Smiling Bobby Eindorf used at the end of the television commercials for his truck and car lot. *"Come on down, it doesn't cost anything to talk."*

At dinner the night before the team left for the tournament, Fenton's mother told him, "Remember to keep your arms inside the window when the bus is moving dear."

His father said when he was growing up he would have given anything to have an experience like Fenton was about to have. "They can take your money but they can't take your memories," he said and smiled as he thought of all Fenton would experience.

His older brother asked if he would bring back a bottle of shampoo from the motel bathroom.

The next morning as the bus pulled away from the Eindorf used car lot, parents waved to their kids who were already playing electronic games or digging through their backpacks for the snacks they'd brought.

They'd traveled a little over an hour when the bus developed engine trouble and pulled off the highway. The driver and one of the parents got out, opened the panel that covered the engine, and poked around, trying to figure out what was wrong.

The cavalcade of parents and school officials who were following the bus stopped long enough to make sure everyone was all right, then continued to Willisburg for the first game of the tournament.

While waiting for a mechanic from Eindorf's to arrive, Coach Barnett had the boys sit in the shade of a large tree and drilled them on, "The mental game of kickball." According to Coach Barnett, "You may not be as good as the other team skill wise BUT if you can out think them," he said as he tapped his head with his finger, "you can beat 'um three ways from Sunday." He told them more games are won by using the six inches of real estate between their ears than with their foot.

He went over game situations and called on different kids to tell him what they would do. "When the infield is pulled in, who backs up the second baseman if the ball is kicked to center field?" Or, "With runners at first and third, what's the sign for a squeeze play?"

Fenton gazed across a grass covered field. Movement caught his eye and soon he was watching a man flying a kite. The kite hung above the tree where the team was seated and he wondered how someone could do that, let the string out and watch the kite swing back and forth, suspended in air.

"...right field? Fenton." Fenton became aware Coach Barnett had called his name. He tried but couldn't come close to guessing the answer to a question he'd asked about something happening in right field. "Well," he said hoping the person next to him would whisper the answer. "I would, I mean, I think in a situation like…"

A horn honked and someone whistled telling the coach it was okay for the boys to get back on the bus, they'd fixed the problem with the motor.

Fenton found his seat and looked out the window to see if the kite was still there. It was and to his surprise he saw the word "**SORRY**" printed on the side facing him.

"What's that about?" Fenton asked louder than he intended and wondered if it had anything to do with his being caught looking at the kite instead of listening to Coach Barnett.

"Huh?" Milton replied to his question. While Fenton was looking at the kite, Milton Eindorf had taken the seat next to him. He dabbed his nose with a tissue while reading a comic book. "You say something?" he asked but kept his eyes on what he was reading.

"Not really," Fenton said as he folded his arms across his chest and slid down in the seat. He sighed when he saw a sign that said Willisburg was still 125 miles away.

When the bus pulled in the circle drive in front of *A Night In Willisburg Motel And Spa,* Coach Barnett stood beside the driver's seat, facing the players. "Boys we lost a chunk of time on the road with the motor problem so you're going to have to take your things to your room and get back out here on the double."

He glanced at his watch and finished with, "We've got ourselves a ball game in exactly twenty minutes so step on it."

When the door to the bus opened the team poured out and ran across the parking lot to their rooms. Fenton found his on the second floor at the end of the hallway. When he got there he was out of breath from carrying the suitcase his mother had packed with extra clothes, "In case you go someplace nice to eat."

He sat down on the bed to rest for a moment.

The phone on the night stand rang.

He didn't know what to do, this was the first time he'd been by himself in a motel room.

He stood, went to the door, and looked out, hoping one of the parents helping their son get settled would tell him what to do but the hallway was empty.

The phone rang.

Fenton picked it up and offered a tentative, "Hello?"

"Ah yes Fenton, this is, ah, Coach Barnett." Fenton thought he heard someone giggle in the background. He'd never actually talked to Coach Barnett on the phone, but the voice sounded familiar.

"Yes Coach? If it's about the question you asked…"

"That's not why I'm calling." Fenton could picture Coach Barnett walking back and forth with his phone pressed to his ear.

The person on the phone was trying not to laugh. "The, ah, bus was blocking the entrance to the motel and we had to move it. So, instead of meeting in front like I told you, we're picking everyone up in back. Got it?"

"Sure, no problem, but I was…" Fenton heard an explosion of laughter from the other end of the phone but before he could ask what was going on, he heard a click.

He glanced at his watch and saw he needed to hurry if he was going to make it to the bus on time. He pulled his ball cap from his suitcase and slipped on the team shirt. He checked to make sure he had the key to his room like his father told him, then closed the door and ran down the hall.

He took the back stairs two at a time and pushed the door open.

He couldn't see Coach Barnett or the bus. Maybe I'm early he thought. "Hey Billy," he called hoping his friend Billy Gilsky was around somewhere.

Billy didn't answer.

"Guys?" The sound of panic rose in his voice as he shouted, "Coach?"

He walked to the edge of the building and looked toward the front driveway in time to see the turn signal on the bus blink on. It stopped for a moment and he was sure someone noticed he was missing and hollered for the driver to wait.

The bus turned onto the street and headed for the ball field.

Fenton sat down on the curb almost in tears.

That's when he thought about the cartoon, the girl holding the football, and the boy lying flat on his back.

Chapter 7
AWAY GAME
Part 2: The Meaning of Air

"I wish I wasn't such a doofus," Fenton muttered as he picked up a rock and threw it at a dumpster in the corner of the parking lot.

He sat down on the curb, put his elbows on his knees, and his face in his hands. What am I going to do now? The bus is gone and won't be back until dark.

Something brushed the bill of his cap and he swatted at it with his hand.

Out of the corner of his eye he saw a shadow, then a kite the shape of a kick ball floated in front of him. "Hi!" was written on its paper surface. Fenton followed the kite string to a man leaning against the dumpster. At first he couldn't remember where he'd seen him, then it came to him. He was the guy in the field when the bus was having engine trouble.

He wore bib overalls and a yellow tee shirt. What hair remained on his head was pulled back in a ponytail. His face was a mass of wrinkles that almost hid his pale blue eyes. He wound the kite string around his hand as he walked across the parking lot.

He sat down next to Fenton but didn't say anything. He reached in a pocket of his overalls and pulled out a business card shaped like a kite and handed it to Fenton. He saw, **Brewster Norwhich,** written in blue letters and below his name was the word, ***Kitest***.

"What's a kitest?" Fenton asked. As he spoke the card wiggled, threatening to break free from his grip.

"I'm not sure it's a word," Brewster spoke so quietly Fenton had to lean towards him to hear. "I made it up but it looks real doesn't it? And when you say it, it sounds real." He rolled and unrolled kite string around his hand as he spoke. "A person who operates a balloon is a balloonist and a piano player is a pianist. So, I figured I fly kites and," he shrugged, "that makes me a kitest."

Fenton nodded. He'd been trying to think of a way to get to the ballpark and explain to Coach Barnett why he missed the bus but with the appearance of Brewster his thoughts had gone in a different direction.

Fenton sighed.

"I know what you mean," Brewster said. His voice sounded so sad Fenton knew he'd had tricks played on him in the past.

They sat together on the curb.

Occasionally Brewster pulled a crumpled piece of paper from his pocket, flattened it, clipped a string on it, and sailed it over the parking lot. Then he'd pull it back, remove the string, wad up the paper, and put it back in his pocket.

Fenton watched in amazement as item after item followed the path of the one before it; a candy wrapper, an aluminum pop can, and finally his ball cap.

"How do you do that?" Fenton asked as Brewster unhooked his cap from the string and put it back on his head. "I can't fly a normal looking kite and you can do it with anything."

"First, you have to know air." Brewster said so matter-of-factly Fenton was sure he'd missed something. Brewster thought about what he said and added, "Once you figure that out the rest is easy."

While he was talking, he pulled a checkered handkerchief from his pocket that was now suspended 20 feet above the parking lot. People walking to their cars stopped and pointed at it. They looked but the string was so thin unless the sun caught it just right even Fenton, who knew where to look, couldn't see it.

"How do you get to know air?" Fenton forgot about missing the bus and was engrossed in questions about air and how something like a ball cap can float on it, or in it, he wasn't sure which.

"Well to start with, it's everywhere." Brewster looked at Fenton to make sure he understood what he was talking about.

Fenton nodded, they'd talked about it in Ms Chalmer's class.

Brewster shrugged, "That's about it."

"That's it?" Fenton felt himself getting angry when he realized Brewster had finished, thinking he'd explained the secret of suspending things in air.

Brewster looked surprised by his reaction. "Oh, you mean beside being everywhere?" A dreamy quality crept into his voice. "It's kind of like walking on the bottom of the ocean only instead of water, there are currents of air and warm spots. Things swim by."

He stood, put out his hand, and motioned for Fenton to join him.

"Feel that?" he asked.

Fenton stuck out his hands, palms down and fingers extended, just like Brewster but didn't feel anything. "No," he said and shook his head, "not really." He felt silly standing in a motel parking lot with his hands in front of him. In fact, he felt pretty silly about the whole thing. He couldn't get Brewster's answers to line up with his questions.

"Seriously?" Brewster seemed surprised. "You didn't feel a pulse of air on your finger tips just then?"

Fenton tried again but shook his head no.

"Over here," Brewster took Fenton's hand and placed it where his had been. Fenton closed his eyes and waited. At first he felt nothing, then there was a gentle push on the tips of his fingers.

"And here," Brewster said excitedly. He moved his hands like he was playing a piano, his fingers rising and falling with each note of air.

Fenton moved where Brewster told him and felt it, just a wisp, like something very small glancing off his fingers.

He looked at the flag on the pole in front of the motel and saw it was hanging straight down, showing no movement. He moved his hands back and forth and danced in circles searching for the slightest breeze and feeling it tug on his fingers.

He turned to tell Brewster he felt it and wondered how he could have missed it but discovered he was gone. The only thing suggesting he'd been there was a piece of string on the curb where they'd been sitting moments before.

Fenton stood when the team bus pulled in the driveway to the motel. It stopped in front of him and when the door opened, he was looking at the angry face of Coach Peewee Barnett.

"Tug," the coach said as he stepped off the bus, "what do you say we have a little talk about following instructions."

As they walked away, Fenton saw the concerned face of Billy Gilsky pressed against a window of the bus.

Fenton and Coach Barnett circled the parking lot Coach Barnett talked about personal responsibility, a chain being no stronger than its weakest link, and there being no I in team. He said he was disappointed in Fenton and something about an apple not falling far from the tree. Fenton had no idea what he was talking about but felt this was not the time to ask questions.

He wanted to tell Coach Barnett about the phone call saying there'd been a change of plans, they were meeting in back of the motel not in front, but once he got started there was no stopping him. He said the team was like a boat and the players had to row together, "Or we'll go in circles."

They were like an airplane grounds crew that had to work together to avoid disaster.

Or the pit crew in an automobile race.

Or a jockey in the Kentucky Derby.

He said playing in a tournament like this was a once in a lifetime opportunity. He'd seen scouts from the Willisburg Vocational School taking notes at the game.

Fenton walked beside him with his head down, looking at the pavement, and nodding occasionally to let him know he was listening.

Coach Barnett said there were kids back in Stemsville that would give their eye teeth to play in a tournament like this. He was sure they wouldn't fritter away the opportunity by missing a bus like Fenton had. If for some strange reason they did, he'd bet dollars to doughnuts they'd crawl on their hands and knees to the ball field if it meant they had a chance to play.

After fifteen minutes of non-stop talking Coach Barnett began to run out of steam. He said he couldn't let Fenton get away with missing the bus and not do anything about it. He had to set an example for this team and the teams he'd coach in the future otherwise they'd think he was a pushover. "If I let one kid get away with something like this, the next thing you know everyone will be doing it.

"To make a long story short," he said as he looked Fenton in the eye, "you're suspended for two games and, unless we win from here on in and advance to the championship round, you'll be watching kickball and not playing it."

Eindorf's Quality Trucks and Cars easily won their first game the next morning and were leading by five runs in the second. The other team had loaded the bases and the kicker was about to take his place behind home plate when his coach called him back to the dugout. Fenton watched him turn the player around and point to right field where Milton Eindorf was crouched down poking the ground with a stick.

The player smiled, nodded he got it, and jogged confidently to home plate.

He kicked the first pitch to right field. Milton got up and chased after the ball. He stopped for a moment when he lost it in the sun, found it, and took off. The ball bounced near the foul line but Milton, moving at full speed, couldn't stop and ran into the pop machine pushed against the outfield fence.

When he stepped away, his glasses were at an odd angle, he had a goofy look on his face, fell over backwards, and didn't move.

A doctor whose grandson was playing for the other team, left the stands and checked him out. He signaled for a stretcher and several spectators helped carry Milton off the field. Everyone stood and clapped, letting him know they appreciated his effort though they thought it was kind of silly for a kid to knock himself out because he hadn't seen something the size of a pop machine.

When he heard the applause, Milton asked if it was raining.

While that was going on, four runs crossed the plate and what had been a comfortable five run lead, had been cut to one.

Fenton scooted forward hoping Coach Barnett would notice he was the only player left on the bench. The coach glanced his way then motioned for the left fielder to move closer to center and the center fielder to move toward right. He would rather play one person short and lose than break his rule that Fenton should sit out two complete games.

The next kicker sent a grounder to the third baseman who fired the ball to first and the game was over. Eindorf's Quality Trucks and Cars was playing for the championship.

The final game of the tournament was a tough one against last year's champion and hometown favorite, the *Willisburg Wings*. Great plays were made by both teams leaving runners stranded on base and keeping the game scoreless going into the last inning.

When it was Eindorf's turn to kick, Billy Gilsky sent a long fly ball to left field but the fielder caught it just before it touched the ground. He gathered the ball in, did a forward role, jumped to his feet, and held it in the air for the umpire to see.

Brian Alexander surprised everyone by bunting the ball toward third but was thrown out when he stumbled over a loose shoestring and lost valuable time in his sprint to first base.

Coach Barnett checked the lineup to see who was up next and to his dismay, discovered it was Fenton. He called for a time out and sent someone to see if Milton felt well enough to play. The messenger returned with a report that Milton said he was okay but wondered why the coach sent three players to ask instead of just one.

Coach Barnett knew he was stuck and reluctantly motioned to Fenton that he was up.

Fenton walked to the plate and went through his pre-kick routine. He tapped the heel of his right sneaker on home plate, tugged on the cuff of his jeans, took two steps behind home plate then turned around to face the pitcher. A quick glance at the outfield showed they were playing him straight away, apparently word of *The Tug Shift* hadn't reached Willisburg.

He was trying to decide if he should kick a line drive down the right field foul line or drop a pop fly behind the short stop when he saw a kite floating above the center field fence. It hung there, with no visible restraint, waiting for the slightest change in the direction of the wind to move it somewhere else

He remembered Brewster and his explanation about air being like the ocean with warm spots and things swimming by. He closed his eyes and held out his hands, palms down, fingers extended, feeling for a breeze or change in air pressure.

He heard something slide by his foot and the umpire yell, "Strike one." Coach Barnett hollered something about this being another of his lame brain ideas and he should stop goofing around and kick the ball like he's supposed to.

The players on the Willisburg Wings laughed and slapped their hands together. Their biggest problem at the moment was finding room in the display case at school for another trophy.

Fenton remained calm, amazingly calm for who he was and the situation he was in. His fingers wiggled and his arms rose and fell, checking for the slightest movement of air.

"Strike two," the umpire hollered then came from behind the catcher and asked if he was the kid who'd run into the pop machine the other day.

He heard Coach Barnett yell, "Why don't you just walk over and hand them the trophy you nitwit." The kids on the bench joined in and asked how much the Willisburg coach was paying him to throw the game.

Bobby Eindorf shouted that Fenton better get his parents to take him home because no quitter was going to ride on his bus. He told the people around him it was the most disgusting show of sportsmanship he'd seen in his life.

The fans of the Willisburg Wings hollered:

Why'd he bother coming?
Why'd he get off the bus?
He should have stayed at home,
and given the trophy to us.

Just when Fenton was about to give up and try to salvage something from the last pitch, he felt it, layers of air stacked on top of one another like tumbling mats in the school gym.

He opened his eyes just as the pitcher released the ball, sending it directly over home plate. After it left his hand, he crouched down, ready to leap in triumph after striking Fenton out with only three pitches, a rare accomplishment in kickball.

Fenton stepped forward and made contact, lifting the ball with the instep of his foot rather then blasting it off his toe. It sailed up and stopped ten feet above the playing field, balanced on a stream of air. The second baseman waited for it to come down but it didn't. The shortstop jumped up and down, swinging his arms wildly, but he was too short to reach it.

Fenton rounded first and headed for second. The ball floated toward the right field foul line and as he stepped on second base, the entire team was grouped together, trying to stand on the shoulders or hands of their teammates in an unsuccessful attempt to reach the ball. The parents of the kids on the team from Willisburg shouted instructions to them and as Fenton ran to third, several left the stands and joined the players on the field. They thought lifting their child to their shoulders would make a difference.

The umpire blew his whistle and waved his arms ordering everyone except the players off the field. No one paid attention to him as they poured from the stand and ran after the ball that floated just out of reach. It dipped down often enough to keep them interested, then rose as a gust of wind sent it back toward first base. The players and fans chased after it with outstretched arms thinking if they could catch the ball before it hit the ground the runner would be out, forcing the game into extra innings.

Fenton stepped on third and turned toward home.

A player for Willisburg took off his shoe and threw it. The ball moved to one side and the shoe fell harmlessly to the ground. Then everyone on the team threw their shoes. The ball bobbed and weaved above their heads like a boxer anticipating where the next punch was coming from.

As Fenton crossed home plate the ball drifted toward center field.

Students at Willisburg Elementary School joined the players and their parents in pursuit of the ball.

The Eindorf Used Trucks and Cars boosters ran on the field and lifted Fenton to their shoulders. The umpire hollered for everyone to get back in the stands, the game wasn't over until the ball returned to the field.

The ball caught an updraft and sailed high in the air until it looked like a dot to those on the ground. Everyone stood with their head back, looking into the sky and wondering what to do while the umpire frantically searched the rule book to see if it covered something like this.

The ball had been airborne for over five minutes.

As quickly as it went up, it came hurtling back to earth. The Willisburg players ran as fast as they could but were slowed by their stocking feet slipping on the grass.

A player made a leaping grab for the ball. He stretched out in midair and grasped the sides but when he hit the ground he lost his grip and watched it bounce away, rolling across the field until it came to rest against the pop machine near the right field foul line.

As Fenton made his way to the bus he walked past Coach Barnett who was telling a reporter form the *Willisburg World* that he, "...never doubted the boy's ability. I wouldn't dream of putting a kid in a pressure packed situation like that if I didn't think he could handle it."

After the first place trophy was presented to the team and pictures taken, the bus pulled away from the curb. Coach Barnett sat in the front with the trophy in the seat next to him.

Fenton was looking out the window when he became aware someone had slid into the seat next to him. He thought it might be Milton and was going to ask how he was feeling; the last time he saw him he was flat on his back, out cold after running into the pop machine.

It wasn't Milton but his father, Bobby Eindorf. "Wonderful job Tug. In all my years playing kickball I've never seen anything like it. If someone told me what happened, I wouldn't believe them." He patted Fenton on the shoulder, handed him a business card, and told him to come down to the car lot, he had something for him.

"Oh," he said as he was getting out of the seat, "be sure to bring your dad along, we might be able to work something out on a van I traded for. Mint condition. Not a scratch. Runs like a top. It's what we call a cream puff."

He continued to the back of the bus where Milton was stretched out across two seats, holding a bag of ice to his head.

Fenton noticed a piece of paper had fallen from Bobby's pocket when he removed his business card. He picked it up and started to tell him he dropped something when he noticed his name written at the top. Beneath it was his room number at the motel and below that, written so quickly it was almost a scrawl he saw, "Change of plans…meet in back, not front."

It took Fenton a moment to figure out it was Bobby Eindorf who'd called his room and not Coach Barnett. Even with a handkerchief over the receiver he couldn't disguise the sound of a salesman trying to talk someone into buying something they didn't want or need.

Oh well, Fenton thought, it worked out okay. If I hadn't missed the bus I wouldn't have met Brewster, learned about air and… He turned away because his eyes filled with tears when he remembered crossing home plate, scoring the winning run, and being congratulated by his teammates. He smiled as he fingered the most valuable player ribbon pinned to his shirt.

He looked out the window to get his mind on something else. It was dusk and long shadows stretched out from trees and smoothed the edges of the mounds in the fields as they rolled by. He was so deep in thought he almost missed it.

A kite hung in the last rays of sunlight. If Coach Barnett had granted one more interview, or they'd waited a moment longer before leaving the ball park, it would have been too dark for him to see it.

He moved closer to the window, studied the back of the kite, and smiled when he saw a circle formed by the words Wish Wizards Inc. And, although he couldn't make it out, he was sure the wishbone of a turkey was in the center of the circle.

I knew they wouldn't let me down," he said softly, sat back in his seat, and closed his eyes. Just before dozing off, he thought of what his father said about no one being able to take away your memories and knew this was one of the rare times he agreed with him.

Chapter 8
TOP BANANA

Fenton Alowishus Tug was mad.

His mother said, "They're temporary dear."

His father told him to keep a stiff upper lip.

His brother Felix popped him on the head with his knuckle, said, "Keep smiling," and laughed at his own joke.

Fenton was so upset about what happened during yesterday's recess he swore he'd never wear his *Kickball Is Life* tee shirt again.

No one made fun of people who don't wear braces.

He wished he could tell his parents what had gone on but it was too embarrassing.

He was standing on first base in a close game, saw the ball blast off Billy Gilsky's foot, watched it sail over the outfielder's head, and realized he could walk to home plate backwards before anyone caught up with it. He was stopped in his tracks when he rounded third and heard the fans of the other team chant:

"He can't run
he's got no shoe laces.
He can't talk
because his teeth have braces."

He stopped, halfway between third and home, unable to move, barely able to breath. It was his first day to wear braces to school, he'd been there exactly two hours and fifteen minutes, and the other team already had a cheer about them. He was thinking about that and the other things that happened that morning when Billy Gilsky, running full speed, rammed him from the back.

As he was getting to his feet Billy said, "What's wrong Tug? Your braces cover your eye teeth so you can't see where you're going?"

Billy laughed.

He said it loud enough for everyone in the stands to hear.

They laughed.

He watched the ball bounce into the outstretched hands of Jimmy Debow the catcher.

"Your out," Jimmy shouted triumphantly.

In more ways than one, Fenton remembered thinking

He excused himself from the table, put his dishes in the sink, and climbed the stairs to his room. "I wish I didn't have to wear these stupid braces," he mumbled partly to himself and partly to anyone who might be listening.

He heard a man's voice. He looked down the hallway but didn't see anyone. He tried to remember if he'd left his radio on when he went downstairs for breakfast. He pushed the door to his room open and found a middle aged man seated at his desk, talking on a mobile phone. He wore a gray pinstriped suit, white shirt, and striped tie. Half glasses were perched on the end of his nose and his black hair, heavy with styling gel, was combed straight back.

The visitor glared at Fenton, said "I'm working here!" and gestured for him to leave.

Fenton apologized, backed out of his room, and closed the door.

He stood in the hallway replaying what just happened. **He'**d been told to leave **his** room by a **complete stranger** sitting at **his** desk and writing in **his** notebook.

Being told to leave his room was the last in a series of disastrous events in his week. He'd had enough and he wasn't going to take it any more. "Not today!" Fenton said quietly. "Not in my house!" He said a little louder as he pushed the door to his room open with such force it banged against the wall and threatened to come back and close.

"What are *you* doing in *my* room?" he demanded.

The visitor stood, turned his back to him, and whispered into his phone, "What's the kid's name? No, I didn't pick up the packet before I left because I was in a meeting until eight and barely made it here on time." The visitor listened, jotted something in Fenton's notebook, and clicked off his phone.

"Ah," he said as he turned toward him, " you must be," he glanced at what he'd written, "Fenton Tug."

Fenton was not about to back down in spite of the visitor's friendly smile and outstretched hand. He was mad when he went to breakfast and his anger moved up a notch when he discovered a complete stranger in **his** room using **his** stuff.

"Yes, I'm Fenton Tug, but **WHO ARE YOU AND WHY ARE YOU MY ROOM?**"

The visitor calmly reached in his vest pocket, removed a business card, and handed it to Fenton just as his phone rang. "Look that over while I take care of this." He flicked a finger at the card and mouthed, "It will explain everything. The card I mean, not the…" he pointed to the phone.

Fenton studied the card and saw the name ***Les Blitz*** printed in gold across the top. ***Vice President of Marketing*** was written beneath his name and below that was a picture of a banana with **Top Banana Entertainment** printed next to it.

"No, I didn't say two graphs," Les moved away from Fenton and spoke quietly into the phone, "I said, two graphs and a chart. Just like the presentation for the Dewhipple account." He looked at Fenton and shrugged, saying with the gesture he was sorry for the interruption and would be finished in a minute.

He turned away and whispered into the phone, "Thanks Darcy, you're a sweetheart." He clicked off the phone and put it in the holster on his belt. "Sorry for the interruption but as they say the clock's ticking, our back's against the wall, and the fat lady is about to sing."

"I don't understand." Fenton said as he pushed his glasses in place and studied the card thinking he'd missed something that would clear things up. Seeing nothing to explain why the stranger was in his room he repeated, "I don't understand."

Les pulled a piece of scotch tape from his trousers, something he'd picked it up while sitting at Fenton's desk, walked over and squatted in front of him.

Fenton wondered if the pennies in his loafers were real.

"Here's the thing," Les said slowly like he was afraid if he talked too fast Fenton wouldn't get it. "Top Banana, the company I work for, is doing promotional work for Wish Wizards, Inc." He paused. "You've heard of them? Wish Wizards, Inc.?"

Fenton nodded he had.

"Fantastic! So I huddled with my focus group, spun the wheel, and it landed on go. I decided to be proactive, put boots on the ground, and become involved in the working end of the operation. I'm going to roll up my sleeves, get my hands dirty, and spend some windshield time with the customer."

He stood, straightened the crease in his trousers, and said proudly. "To make a long story short and cut to the chase, I'm your wish wizard."

Fenton blinked.

"Once I see how things work," Les said as he walked to the window, pulled back the curtain, and looked in the backyard, "I'll make a few changes, rearrange the organizational furniture, and get management to color outside the lines."

He spun around and Fenton felt he'd become part of a larger audience. "**URC**," he said and held up his index finger, "UNDERSTAND." He stuck his thumb in the air, "REFLECT," he said the word with an emphasis on the RE. "And, last but not least," a third finger joined the other two, "CHANGE. **UNDERSTAND. REFLECT. CHANGE.** Three words that pulled Top Banana out of the small business swamp, placed it at the pinnacle of the entertainment field, and made it a household word." When he finished he was standing with a foot on the seat of Fenton's chair and a finger pointing at the ceiling.

He paused, lowered his voice and said, "Without **URC**, Top Banana would just be one of the bunch." He waited for Fenton to laugh at a joke he'd told hundreds of times. When he didn't he continued. "You've heard of Top Banana?" He asked in a way that suggested he was sure the answer was yes.

Fenton shook his head no.

Les shrugged and mumbled, "You win some, you lose some."

"**YOU DON'T GET IT. YOU DON'T…**" Fenton had to stop because tears filled his eyes and his chin began to quiver.

"I don't need Top Banana. I don't need a Vice President of Marketing. I need someone with dental experience. I need…"

"URC!" Les repeated the term he'd used earlier.

Someone knocked on the door. Les gestured for Fenton to stay where he was, opened the door, and mumbled something to whoever was in the hallway. Then, after receiving several large sheets of paper and a wooden easel, he closed the door.

He set the easel next to Fenton's desk and placed the sheets of paper on it.

Across the top of the first paper Fenton read, "**FENTON TUG POPULARITY STUDY OVER A 9 MONTH PERIOD. MS CHALMER'S CLASS. SEPTEMBER TO MAY.**"

Below the heading were things that looked like tubes placed next to each other. Under each tube was the name of a month starting with September on the left and ending with May on the right. Going up the left side of the page were numbers with zero on the bottom and ten at the top.

Fenton examined the tubes. It looked like someone had poured red ink in them, they were filled to the number three. Next to the number six was a blue line with a star beside it. He started to ask what it meant but stopped when he saw another star at the bottom of the paper with "***POPULARITY LEVEL OF THE AVERAGE 3rd GRADE STUDENT**" next to it.

"Do you know what this is?" Les asked, pointing to the chart.

"Well sure," Fenton bobbed his head and tapped his foot while he studied the paper, "it's a graph or something?"

"**Awesome!**" Les seemed pleased. "Now, what does the graph or something tell us?"

Fenton studied the gap between the top of the red ink in the tubes and the blue line with the star by it. He sighed when he saw how far below average he was.

"Exactly," Les said as if reading his thoughts.

Fenton noticed the red ink was nearly touching the blue line in the September tube. What had he done in…his birthday was in September and his mother made cupcakes for the class. He sat on his bed, overcome by the message of the graph; he hadn't made it to average by a long way.

"U." Les said dramatically, "UNDERSTAND."

He pulled the top sheet off the easel and sailed it across the room.

The second paper had one tube and was full of red ink; only a sliver of white showed at the top.

Printed across the bottom of the page was, **FENTON TUG POPULARITY STUDY April 9th.**

Fenton thought for a minute, checked the calendar on his desk, saw it was Saturday, April 7th. and said, "Hold on a second, that's *next* Monday."

"The result of our latest projection," Les said proudly.

Fenton looked at the ink in the tube. It was obvious he was going to be a very popular guy on Monday. He squinted and studied the small space between the ink and the top of the tube, pointed to it, and looked a question at Les.

"*Almost* everyone will like you Fenton, isn't that enough?" Les asked and raised an eyebrow.

Fenton sighed and nodded yes. He noticed with pride how far the top of the red ink was above the blue line.

Les pulled that paper off the easel, dropped it on the floor, and a new page faced Fenton.

"**R**," Les said solemnly, then turned to the easel. Across the top of the paper, in blue letters he saw, **DEWHIPPLE REPORT**. His shoulders sagged. He yanked the phone from his belt, punched in a number and said, "Darcy. Sweetheart. I said **like** the Dewhipple report not **the** Dewhipple report." He hit the end button.

Fenton heard a knock on the door. Les walked across the room, opened it, and stepped in the hallway. He returned carrying another piece of paper. Before closing the door he said, "You're the best," to whoever was outside, then retraced his steps and put the paper on the easel.

Fenton froze.

Written in large letters, filling the entire page he saw:

He can't run
he's got no shoe laces.
He can't talk
because his teeth have braces.

"**R**," Les said in a serious tone after giving Fenton a moment to study the page. "**REFLECT**."

He waited while Fenton read it a second time.

When he was sure he understood what was written there Les said, "I want to ask a few questions." Les paced in front of Fenton, with his hands clasped behind his back. "AND," he let the word hang in the air until he was sure Fenton was listening. "I want you to answer yes or no. I don't want, I guess or whatever. Simply answer the question yes or no. Can you do that?"

Fenton shrugged.

"Yes or no Fenton?"

"Yes." When he said it, Fenton felt the atmosphere in the room change.

"Okay now," Les pointed to the second line of the chart, "do your shoes have laces?"

"Yes," from Fenton who after saying it, stood a little taller.

Les's finger moved up a line. "And, now that we've confirmed beyond a shadow of doubt your shoes have laces, can you run?"

"Yes." Fenton was so excited he almost said it before Les finished.

"I want you to think carefully before answering this very important question." He waited until he was sure Fenton was ready then said, "Even though your teeth have braces, can you talk?"

"Yes!" Fenton hollered.

"Yes!" He yelled as he jumped on his bed.

"Yes!" He said, each time his feet touched the mattress.

"So," Les said as Fenton continued bouncing and saying yes. "If what they said isn't true..." Fenton stopped somewhere between the high point of his jump and the top of the mattress when he heard him ask, "What's the big deal?"

Fenton's feet came to rest on his bed and he fell over backwards. He stared at the ceiling, out of breath and too stunned to talk. Nothing the crowd said was true. His shoes had laces and he could run. And yes he had braces but he could talk. Why hadn't he thought of it himself? Why did it take the

Vice President of Marketing for Top Banana Entertainment to point it out? And, if it wasn't true, what was the big deal?

He turned to say something but discovered, while he had been thinking about laces and braces, Les had gone and taken the easel and papers with him. The only indication he'd been in the room was a small piece of scotch tape stuck to the edge of his desk.

Monday morning, October 9th, Fenton was sitting on his bed, completely dressed. He was wearing his newest shoes, his best jeans, and his *Kickball Is Life* tee shirt waiting for his mother to knock on the door, letting him know breakfast would be ready in five minutes.

After breakfast he picked up his lunch box and backpack. He got a kiss from his mother, a pat on the back from his father, and dodged a pop on the head by his brother as he ran out the door. He couldn't wait to get to school and find out what was going to happen that would make him so popular.

The ride on the bus was over in seconds and before he knew it, it was time to walk single file to the school entrance.

He sat on the edge of his chair during the first two hours of class wondering if giving the correct answer to a difficult question was going to be the turning point for him. By the time morning recess rolled around Ms Chalmer hadn't called on him once.

He was picked next to last when they chose kick ball teams, beating out Billy Gilsky because he told someone he had a stomach ache.

When it was his turn to kick he stepped to the plate and hollered for the pitcher to roll the ball, "Slow and smooth."

While he waited, he glanced at the fans of the other team and noticed a wooden easel holding a large piece of paper in front of the bleachers. He saw Les Blitz standing at the edge of the cheering mob. He was wearing the same suit he had on when he appeared in his room and held a pointer in his hand. He gave a thumbs up sign to Fenton and winked, suggesting he knew something Fenton didn't.

Fenton said yes quietly to himself as the ball approached. He said yes again as he took a step forward and planted his left foot. He said, "**YES**," out loud as he brought his right foot through, catching the ball on the toe of his shoe. He watched in amazement as the ball took off like a shot, sailed over the head of the second baseman, and through the outstretched arms of Myron Clugg, the left fielder.

He watched Myron turn, start to run after the ball then slow to a walk when he realized there was no way he could reach it before Fenton crossed home plate. The ball came to rest next to the phone booth at the far end of the playground.

Fenton skipped to first base, jogged past second and made the turn at third. He slowed when he saw Les step in front of the crowd and direct their attention to the paper on the easel.

"Fenton Tug
will be looking great,"

the fans of the other team yelled as they followed the pointer,

"when the braces come off
and his teeth are straight."

Fenton made a final jump and landed on home plate.

Fans of his team cheered. Fans of the other team clapped their hands and whistled. His teammates pounded him on his back and hollered, "Great kick Tug."

Fenton stood on home plate after everyone had picked up their lunch boxes and coats and walked back to their classroom, their cheers still echoing in his ears.

This, he thought after scoring the only run of the game, is the best day of my life.

He walked through the outfield, past the picnic table, and up the path that took him back to school and Ms Chalmer's room.

The phone by the picnic table rang. He looked around but didn't see anyone waiting for a call.

He walked over to the phone booth and waited.

It rang again.

He checked, thinking he might have missed someone but there was no one in sight.

The phone rang.

Fenton lifted the receiver off the hook and said, "Hello?"

"Fenton, sweetheart, it's Les Blitz from Top Banana. How's your day going?"

"Wonderful," Fenton answered. "The best ever." He was afraid to say more, he was so happy he thought he'd cry if he did.

"Top shelf," Les said and waited a moment before moving to the reason for his call. "Here's the thing Fenton. I'm headed to Tulsa, Oklahoma for a seminar on, *The Future of Kettle Corn in Dinner Theaters* and I wanted to touch base with you before I left."

"Les, about Wish Wizards, Inc. are you gong to change anything? You know, **URC**?"

He heard Les tell someone he'd be with them in a minute, then he was back.

"Is your notebook handy?"

"Yeah, I mean, yes."

"I want to be up front with you. No tricks up my sleeve. No hocus-pocus. No now you see it, now you don't. Sometimes you change things, do you see where I'm going with this? And sometime," he paused and to emphasize how important this point was he repeated, "sometime," before finishing with, "you leave them alone. You with me Fenton?"

Fenton nodded he was.

Les continued, "So here's what I want you to do. Do you have a pencil?"

Fenton nodded he did.

"Do you have a clean piece of paper? One that's not folded or scribbled on?"

Fenton nodded he was ready.

"Outstanding! Now write the letters **U** and **R** like you've seen in my presentation but instead of putting **C** at the end, add the letters **O** and **K**. Because sometimes things are okay just the way they are. Did you get all of that?"

"I think so." Fenton mumbled as he finished writing the K.

"Read it back to me." Fenton heard footsteps, like Les was jogging down a long hallway.

He read it out loud, "**U.R.O.K**." Then asked, "Did I get it right?"

Les said, "Over the fence. Nothing but net. Now do me a favor?"

"Sure."

"Put the piece of paper by your bed and read it when you get up in the morning. Will you do that for me?"

"No problem."

Fenton heard a woman say, "You have to turn off your phone sir." That was followed by Les saying, "Ciao," and then a click.

Fenton hung up the phone and looked at the paper.

He scratched his head.

He thought for a moment then said the letters quietly to himself, **"U.R.O.K."** He remembered Les saying sometimes things were okay just the way they were.

He took off for Ms Chalmer's room, not wanting to miss a moment of the best day of his life.

Chapter 9
AFTERMATH

Fenton Alowishus Tug was nervous.

His mother told him to, "Solve one problem at a time dear."

His father looked over the top of his newspaper and said, "No pressure, no diamonds."

His older brother Felix saw the worried look on his face and went straight to his place at the table without popping him on the head with his knuckle.

Fenton was sure Brian Alexander didn't have a care in the world this weekend.

He knew Perky Bergbinder, who'd skipped two grades and was being considered for a third, would be spending Saturday at the library like he usually did.

Fenton picked up his bowl and carried it to the sink.

His mother whispered, "He barely touched his food."

His father replied, "He's a Tug, he'll figure it out."

His brother pointed with his spoon and said, "If he doesn't come back can I have his raisin toast?"

Fenton went to his room, pulled a sheet of paper and pencil from the top drawer of his desk, and started to work the example problems in the back of his arithmetic book. The first one didn't make sense so he gave the second a try but didn't do any better with it.

He thought about yesterday's recess.

He'd been told to play right field by Billy Gilsky the team captain. "Don't worry," Billy told him as they jogged to their place in the outfield, "nobody kicks the ball to right field."

The first guy up kicked the ball to right field.

"All yours," Billy called.

Fenton kept his eye on the ball as he ran toward the foul line and was surprised when he tripped over Perky Bergbinder.

Perky is the smartest kid in the third grade, maybe the smartest kid in the world. His name is Percival Booth Bergbinder the 3rd but everybody calls him Perky, or Perky the Brain, or Perky the Boy Genius.

When he was in kindergarten he brought the ingredients for a stink bomb to school and talked Billy Gilsky into mixing them together. When they finally cleared the smell from the building and allowed the children back in, Principal Logan sent Billy home for two days to think about what he'd done. He told him to decide if he wanted to be a student at Buffalo Bill Cody Elementary or go someplace else. The way he said it suggested he wouldn't take it personally if he chose to go to a different school.

When he was allowed to return, Billy spent a week of valuable recess time writing, *"I will not bring a stink bomb to school,"* on the chalk board. Perky's roll in the event had gone unnoticed and, in spite of the injustice of it, Billy Gilsky had been true to the kindergarten code; never tell on a classmate.

When he was in first grade, Perky hacked into the school computer system. This time he didn't get off as easy. It was obvious to the office staff who the culprit was because he changed everyone's gym grade to **F** for Failing except his, which became **O** for Outstanding. Coach Peewee Barnett told Principal Logan, "It's got Perky's fingerprints all over it. The boy couldn't do a push up if his life depended on it."

As Fenton got to his feet he noticed Perky had been drawing with a stick in one of the few places on the field not covered with grass. He studied the drawing and saw a triangle with little blocks stacked on each side.

Perky straightened his glasses, brushed the dirt off his pants and when he saw Fenton looking at what he'd drawn said, "Pythagoras."

"Wha...?" was all Fenton could think of to say.

"The Pythagorean theorem." Perky added thinking it would clear things up. "I proved he was right."

"Oh," Fenton tried to sound like he knew what he was talking about, "the ah, triangle guy?"

Later in the day Fenton learned that he and Dorthea Simmons would represent Ms Chalmer's class in *AfterMath*. *AfterMath* is the brainchild of Mr. Dice, fifth grade science teacher and faculty adviser for *Math-A-Maniacs,* the school math club. Since Perky had become eligible to join them, they'd not only dominated every school competition but had been city champs two years in a row.

After failing to solve a third problem, Fenton pushed the arithmetic book aside and put his arms on his desk. He laid his head on his arms and whispered in a voice on the verge of tears, "I wish I didn't have a math problem."

He closed his eyes.

He heard the door to his room open and close.

He smelled soap and someone said, "If Master Fenton would slip on this robe, I have taken the liberty of drawing your bath." He saw his plaid robe folded over the arm of someone his grandfather's age. He wore a dark blue suit, white shirt, and a gray and white striped tie. Fenton could see his reflection in the visitor's shoes.

Fenton stammered, "You did what?"

"I've taken the liberty of preparing your bath and will return when it's ready." The visitor turned to go.

"Wait, hold on a second," Fenton protested. "You may not have noticed but it's Saturday. I never take a bath on Saturday." He wasn't particularly fond of baths and couldn't see wasting time taking one when he didn't have to.

"That explains it then," the visitor said.

"Explains what? I was…" Fenton lifted his hands hoping to convey he hadn't the slightest idea what the stranger was talking about.

"The note on my assignment slip." The visitor said as he picked a piece of lint from the sleeve of Fenton's sweatshirt.

"What note? What assignment slip? What…?" Fenton couldn't think of anything else to ask.

"Here sir, in black and white." The visitor pulled a computerized form from his pocket, unfolded it, and read the top line. "*Wish Assignment: Fenton Alowishus Tug.* And, if I may direct your attention to what is written below your name," he pointed to the middle of the page and read, "**Client Request**: *Wishes he didn't have a bath problem.*"

He waited for Fenton to read it before asking, "Do you deny saying it sir?"

Fenton studied the paper and mumbled, "Bath problem?" He thought for a moment then it came to him. "Okay," he took a step toward the visitor. "Hold on. I get it. There's been a mistake, ah, what's your name?"

"Benton," he answered.

"Well Benton, I don't have a **bath** problem, I have a **math** problem. Whoever took the message wrote it down wrong."

"Whatever you say sir." Benton laid the robe on the edge of Fenton's bed. "Your bath should be ready now."

"Whoa, hold on a minute. Let me explain something... you're Benton the Butler?" Fenton asked.

"Valet sir."

"Butler, valet, whatever." It was obvious from the tone in Fenton's voice he was upset.

"A butler," Benton explained, "takes care of the house while a valet," he paused before saying, "takes care of the master of the house which, in this case, is you."

"You don't understand Benton? I am going to be destroyed in a math contest on Monday. The way it stands now, if I go without sleep, don't eat, and stay at my desk working math problems all weekend, I'm sill going to get creamed."

"I have discovered Master Fenton things look more promising after a hot bath." Benton paused before saying, "Trust me on this one sir."

"Fenton," his mother called from the bottom of the stairs, "are you running bath water?"

"Kind of," Fenton told her.

"It's Saturday dear," his mother reminded him and added in a concerned voice, "are you feeling okay?"

"Kind of," Fenton answered.

"I knew something was wrong," she said as she hurried away to find his father.

Twenty minutes later, after soaking in the bathtub, Fenton, was wrapped in his bathrobe and stretched out on his bed. Benton sat in the chair by the desk.

"...besides that, Perky's a genius so..." Fenton was rambling, saying whatever popped in his mind.

"It's not easy being a genius, sir, " Benton offered. "Their life is not the bed of roses people think it is. I was the personal valet to Dr. J. Norfleet Schroder for a number of years. Perhaps you've heard of his groundbreaking work with the German cockroach?"

He studied Fenton's face for some sign that he'd heard of his former employer.

Fenton shook his head but thought the part about the cockroach sounded interesting.

Benton continued. "He worked for years with one tribe eventually discovering the key to communicating with one them. There were additional years learning to imitate their squeaks and chirps. Eventually, using their language, he taught them a few simple tricks like standing on their back legs and, what proved to be very difficult for a cockroach, a forward roll.

"But, as intelligent as he was, Dr. Schroder could not master the most basic requirements for living. He never learned how to tie his shoes," Fenton remembered the Velcro straps across the top of Perky's sneakers. "Or comb his hair," Benton shook his head to emphasize the point. "No, Master Fenton, take my word for it, it's not easy being a genius, especially for one as young as Percival."

"We're not talking about cockroaches Benton, this is arithmatic. Perky knows all about trigonometry. He proved Pythagoras was right." The more Fenton talked about Perky's accomplishments the more he felt tension creep into his neck and shoulders.

He wondered if he should take another bath.

Benton raised a finger, pressed it against his lips, and looked at a place above Fenton's head.

"Are you okay?" Fenton asked.

"I was trying to recall something Dr. Schroder said." Benton tilted his head and after a moment stuck a finger in the air. "I have it now sir. He often said, 'If I had enough time, I could teach a pig to use a napkin.'"

"What has that got to do with any…"

"A random thought Master Fenton," Benton explained, "one must give way to random thoughts from time to time."

"Has Master Fenton decided what he is going to wear to school today?"

"I, ah, what time…" Fenton was barely awake. He looked out the window and saw it was still dark. He heard his Mother turn the light on in the kitchen and knew it would be another ten minutes before she knocked on his door.

"Did you say something about…" Fenton hadn't reached the point where he was thinking about clothes, he was trying to figure out what day it was. When he remembered it was Monday, he fell back on his bed and moaned, "This is the day I get destroyed."

"I've taken the liberty of laying out a few things Master Fenton," Benton said as he fluffed the pillows on Fenton's bed, "Your khaki slacks, a collared tee shirt, and this attractive sweater vest."

"Whatever," Fenton muttered as he rolled out of bed and headed for the bathroom.

When he walked in the kitchen his mother greeted him with, "Today's the big day."

"When the going gets tough the Tugs get tougher," his father said as he turned a page of the morning newspaper,

His brother said, "I didn't make it out of the first round when I was in third grade. I still have bad dreams about it."

"Thanks," Fenton said as he picked his lunch box off the counter and walked out of the kitchen.

The bus didn't have a flat tire so it wasn't late picking him up like he'd hoped.

The engine didn't explode as they pulled away from the curb, which messed up his back up plan.

A car didn't swerve out of control and smash into the side of the bus as Fenton had pictured and, without a flat tire, explosion or collision, he saw his chance of missing the contest go down the drain.

He was the last to leave when the bus pulled into its parking place. He watched with envy as the other students headed to their classrooms; it was just another school day for them.

When he opened the door to the auditorium it felt like he was entering a war zone. Supporters from each class stood face to face, yelling what their representatives would do to their opponents.

Mr. Dice was on stage and when he saw Fenton he motioned for him to join the other contestants on stage.

"Let's have some order," Mr. Dice said and tapped the microphone to make sure it was on.

Gradually the noise died down and the students returned to their seats.

When it was finally quiet Mr. Dice, wearing a white lab coat, his trademark at Cody Elementary, leaned closer to the microphone. Fenton glanced over and noticed Mitzi Donnell had been chosen as Perky's partner, like he needed help.

He looked at the audience and saw Perky's father sitting with his son's class. He was an exact duplicate of Perky only a little older. If it wasn't for his nicely trimmed mustache and beard they could have passed as brothers instead of father and son.

"You know how the contest works," Mr. Dice slipped into his teacher voice and Fenton fought the urge to take notes. "Questions are selected from four different categories; Math Facts, Going the Distance, Fantastic Fractions, and a new category this year, Random Numbers."

A chant started from Perky's class:

> *"Give him the gold,*
> *give him the cup,*
> *Perky's going to win,*
> *when the score is added up."*

When they finished they stomped their feet and clapped their hands. Fenton noticed Perky's father facing the audience, encouraging them to join in.

Mr. Dice stood at the podium and smiled, allowing the demonstration to continue.

Then Fenton heard the members of *Math-A-Maniacs* say:

> *"Don't worry Perky,*
> *Fenton can't add,*
> *division is a mystery,*
> *and his subtraction's really bad."*

Ms Chalmer stood to object and Mr. Dice held up his hand to quiet the crowd. "Now Mildred," he said, "they're just blowing off a little steam. Your class will be given equal time."

A hush fell over the auditorium. The students were stunned. It was like a crack suddenly appeared in the wall separating them from their teachers. No one knew her first name was Mildred and somehow they felt they weren't supposed to. As far as they were concerned, teachers didn't have first names. They were either Ms, Mrs., or Mr. and that's all there was to it.

"I mean, ah, Ms Chalmer," Mr. Dice stammered, hoping to cover up what he said. Fenton wondered if it was a mistake or if he'd done it on purpose to throw the contestants off.

"To make sure each of the candidates has equal time," Mr. Dice continued, still blushing from calling Ms Chalmer by her first name, "would someone in Ms Chalmer's room like to say a few words?"

At first he didn't see Billy Gilsky's raised hand. When he did, he pointed and wiggled his fingers, indicating he could start any time.

Billy stood and tugged on a sleeve of his sweater. "Well, I'm like, Billy Gilsky, a third grader in Mildred's," he stopped and his face turned red. "I mean Ms Chalmer's room." He turned and pointed in her direction in case someone in the auditorium didn't know who she was.

Mr. Dice looked at his watch and rolled his hand indicating Billy needed to wrap things up, he was wasting valuable time.

"What? Oh, I see. Sure. No problem. Fenton," Billy struggled with what to say next, "don't mess up and embarrass our class okay?" He gave a quick bow and returned to his seat. Those around him patted him on the back and told him he'd done a good job.

"I've asked Doctor Bergbinder, Perky's father, to help this morning." Mr. Dice stretched out his hand inviting him to the stage. "He is the Professor of Applied Science and Mathematics at Stemsville Technical College and will draw numbers from a hat to determine the order in which the questions will be asked."

When the drawing was finished, it was determined that Mitzi would go first, followed by Dorthea, Perky, and finally Fenton. Luck of the draw, Fenton thought to himself.

Mitzi dropped out in the second round when, after picking *Fantastic Fractions* and failing to add two of them correctly.

Dorthea chose, *Going The Distance*, as her category in round three. Mister Dice removed a card from the folder and read, "A man hits a ball 93 yards with his 9 iron. How far is that in feet and inches?" He turned the card over, looked at Dorthea, and started the timer.

Dorthea panicked.

"What's a 9 iron?" She asked Fenton but he couldn't help or he'd be disqualified.

"What's a 9 iron?" She asked her class but none of them knew. She jumped when the buzzer sounded indicating her time was up.

"What's a 9 iron?" She asked through tears as she made her way to her seat beside her parents. When she sat down her mother put an arm around her quivering shoulders. Her father gripped his hands like he was holding a golf club and swung at an imaginary ball.

"Oh," she said between sobs, "that 9 iron."

"Reverse order," Perky said so casually Fenton thought he asked for a glass of water.

"Perky has called for a reverse order," Mr. Dice explained to the curious audience. "It is a seldom used strategy in the *AfterMath* contest, but perfectly legal according to the rules as they are written. Reverse order simply means I will ask a question from a category Fenton selects. If," he paused to make sure the audience understood how reverse order worked, "Perky answers the question correctly, he wins this years contest."

Fenton heard a murmur run through the crowd. They didn't understand everything Mr. Dice said but they caught enough to know Perky could win it all by answering one question.

Fenton saw Perky's Father wink and give him the thumbs up sign letting him know he was proud he was able to think clearly under pressure.

A picture formed in Fenton's mind of a pig dabbing at the corner of his mouth with a napkin and he remembered what Benton said about random thoughts.

"Random Numbers Mr. Dice," Fenton said but wasn't sure why.

"Perky," Mr. Dice said solemnly, " the subject is Random Numbers."

Perky took his time walking to the microphone. It was like he did it every day so it was no big deal. When he got there, he nodded he was ready.

Mr. Dice removed a card, read it, put it back and started to draw another.

"**MR. DICE!**" Every kid in the room heard the tone in Ms Chalmer's voice and breathed easier when they realized she hadn't called their name.

Mr. Dice looked embarrassed, drew back his hand, and read the card, "How many outs are made when a triple play is completed in a kickball game?"

The look of confidence on Perky's face so evident moments before, was gone. He seemed to shrink in size and Fenton noticed beads of perspiration appear on his forehead. He saw Professor Bergbinder inch forward in his seat.

"**Percival. Booth. Bergbinder.**" Mr. Dice said slowly emphasizing each name and hoping Perky could take it a step farther and add **the 3rd**. He'd made up his mind he would accept third as an answer if Perky was able to make the connection.

Ms Chalmer figured out what was going on and stood to object. When she saw the blank look on Perky's face she realized he couldn't have answered if the question had been, "What is your name?"

"Ah," Perky tugged nervously on the collar of his shirt, looked at Mr. Dice and said, "Two? Or maybe…" just before the buzzer sounded.

Fenton heard a gasp from the *Math-A-Maniacs*.

He doubted Perky had ever played kickball, baseball, or anything involving a ball in his life and couldn't imagine what that would be like. He thought how odd the question to determine the winner of *AfterMath* had come down to one so simple any normal kid could answer it with their eyes closed.

"**MY SON IS A NITWIT!**" Perky's father yelled as he wadded up the *AfterMath* program he'd been holding and threw it on the ground. "**I'M RAISING A KNUCKLEHEAD! A NINCOMPOOP! A COMPLETE AND TOTAL DOOFUS!**" He continued shouting as he pushed his way down the row of seats toward the aisle. "**THINK ABOUT IT PERCIVAL. A *TRIPLE* PLAY. A *TRIPLE* ANYTHING.**"

"**YOU'LL ANSWER FOR THIS WHEN YOU GET HOME YOUNG MAN,**" he hollered as he hurried up the aisle. When he reached the auditorium door he turned to say something else. He shook his head and mumbled he couldn't understand how anyone in their right mind could miss a question like that.

He slammed the door when he left.

Perky sat down on the folding chair and buried his face in his hands. He was humiliated by not knowing the answer and his father's outburst. Fenton saw his shoulders shake and thought he heard a sob.

Mr. Dice fought to keep the disappointment from his voice when he said, "Your turn Tug?" Fenton was sure he was thinking, of all the kids in Buffalo Bill Cody Elementary why did it have to be Fenton? And why did the question to determine the winner of this year's *AfterMath* have to be about kickball?

Fenton stood and walked to the microphone.

"Do you know the answer?" Mr. Dice said it in a way that reminded Fenton of a parent asking a kid if he wanted an ice cream cone. The answer was so obvious, it would have been simpler if Mr. Dice forgot the question and handed him the *AfterMath* trophy.

Fenton closed his eyes and pictured the glass fronted case in the entry hall of the school where they kept the *Aftermath* trophy. On top of the trophy was the brass figure of a student, sitting at a school desk with his hand raised, eager to answer whatever question had been asked. The name of every student who'd won the contest was engraved on the front and, in a few moments, if he played his cards right, his would join theirs.

He stood at the microphone and the boys in Ms Chalmer's class moved to the edge of their seat, ready to leap in the air and celebrate when he gave the answer. They couldn't believe one of their own, an ordinary kid they played kickball with every recess, was about to win the *Aftermath* contest.

The *Math-A-Maniacs* were huddled together trying to figure out what a kickball was.

It grew quiet when it looked like Fenton was about to answer.

"I agree with Perky Mr. Dice," Fenton said, "the correct answer is two."

The boys in Ms Chalmer's class looked at each other in disbelief. Was this the Fenton Tug who lived and breathed kickball? Was this the Fenton Tug who had more *Kickball Hero* trading cards than anyone in school?

No one in his class said a word as they stood, formed two lines, and marched quietly out of the auditorium. Before leaving, Ms Chalmer glanced toward the stage, made sure Fenton was watching and smiled, letting him know she understood what he'd done.

Perky lifted his head and looked at Fenton through tear filled eyes.

Fenton sat down next to him, shrugged, and said, "It was a random thought."

Soon the auditorium was empty of everyone except Fenton who remained seated in the folding chair, swinging his legs back and forth.

He smelled soap.

"Well done Master Fenton, Dr. Schroder would be proud." Benton said from the back of the auditorium. "It looks like the dispatcher at Wish Wizards Inc. was right about what she put on my assignment sheet."

Fenton looked up, puzzled.

"If I might say sir, you don't have a math problem. At least as far as I can tell."

Fenton sighed. He could have named the top five triple play combinations in the world if there'd been a follow up question. But as he was about to answer he thought of Perky going home empty handed and his father yelling at him.

He thought about how close he'd come to leaving something behind that said he'd been a student here.

His thoughts were interrupted when Benton asked, "What is on your schedule for the rest of the day Master Fenton?"

Fenton walked to the microphone at the center of the stage, leaned in to it and said, "When I get home from school, I plan to take a long, hot bath."

To Fenton's surprise he saw something he thought he'd never see. It was better than winning the contest and having his name engraved on the *AfterMath* trophy.

Benton the valet was smiling.

Chapter 10
THIRD GRADE DANCE

Fenton Alowishus Tug was afraid to move.

Dorthea Simmons was standing uncomfortably close.

He was surrounded by the members of Ms Chalmer's third grade class who were watching every move he made.

Do something, he told himself. His class had been to the gym several times to practice but with everyone watching and Dorthea looking at him expectantly, he forgot everything he'd learned. If it had been The Third Grade Kickball Tournament *he'd know exactly what to do.*

Dorthea Simmons was not interested in kickball, she was waiting for him to take her in his arms and dance.

His mother said, "It's where I met your father."

Fenton blinked. He was at the breakfast table but where had his mind been? Something about Dorthea Simmons? None of it made sense to him.

His father lowered his newspaper and filled in a few details his mother had left out. "Horace Gorman was supposed to be her partner but we traded numbers and I danced with her instead."

His brother Felix mumbled, "I had the chicken pox so I missed it." Before taking a bite of his English muffin he added, "Pretty good timing I'd say."

The Third Grade Dance is an event organized by Ms Chalmer and Mrs. Brubaker. Every year, since before Fenton's parents attended Buffalo Bill Cody Elementary, they'd sponsored the dance. They combined their classes, drew names for partners and, on the first Monday in April, the last two hours of school were spent in the gymnasium dancing.

"We're getting them ready for middle school," Mrs. Brubaker explained to Mary Jane Thompson's mother who'd asked if it wasn't a little early for girls her daughters age to be dancing with boys.

Ms Chalmer added, "We're teaching them what to do when faced with," she made quote marks in the air, "*a real dance scenario.* Suits. Dresses. Flowers. The whole ball of wax." Her eyes filled with tears and she finished with, "It's an experience they'll never forget."

Mrs. Brubaker nodded enthusiastically, letting Mrs. Thompson know her daughter was in good hands.

Fenton became suspicious when, right after the numbers that matched partners for the dance had been passed out, Sally Graves from Mrs. Brubaker's class asked if she could use the pencil sharpener in Ms Chalmer's room. "Ours broke," she explained as she took the long way to the sharpener. When she finished, she went back the other way, making a complete tour of the room. Fenton watched her scan the top of the boy's desks, hoping to see the scraps of paper with numbers on them as she made her way to the door.

Sally Graves has a terrific memory.

At recess that afternoon he saw the girls huddled by the kickball backstop with Sally in the center. They were passing pieces of paper back and forth, exchanging partners for the dance. So much for the luck of the draw he remembered thinking.

"I think I'm supposed to get a flower or something," Fenton mumbled.

"It's called a corsage dear," his mother said dreamily.

"While were out, we could look for ballet shoes in your size," his father said and chuckled.

"Or track shoes," his brother added. Fenton watched as they reached across the table and bumped fists.

"May I be excused?" Fenton asked and carried his dishes to the sink.

"He could meet his true love," his mother sighed.

"You had me after the first dance," his father told her and patted her hand.

"Would you knock off the lovey-dovey stuff," his brother groaned, "I'm still eating."

Fenton went to the family room and plopped down on the sofa. He picked at the fabric and said, "I wish I didn't have to go to the stupid dance."

He sat back and closed his eyes.

He heard heavy footsteps coming across the family room. He opened his eyes and expected to see his father and brother had come to kid him some more about the dance. Instead, he saw a large man wearing green coveralls, work boots, and a stocking cap striding toward him. Even though he was several feet away, Fenton could smell something like…garbage?

The visitor got so close Fenton had to lean back to keep from bumping heads.

"You want a piece of me?" The visitor shouted. **"Well it better be a big piece because I, ah,** because…awe shucks, I forgot my line."

He sat down on the footstool next to the couch, pulled a paper from his back pocket, and studied it.

"Are you sure you're in the right house?" Fenton asked hesitantly.

"You're Tug, right? Fenton A?" The visitor asked but didn't look up from the paper he was reading.

"Yes, but, I..." Fenton wasn't prepared for his answer. He expected an apology and an embarrassed departure by the visitor, hopefully leaving the same way he came so his parents wouldn't know he'd been there.

"Roscoe Bean," the stranger said and pushed a beefy hand toward Fenton. "A.K.A. *The Garbage Man.*"

"I don't..." from Fenton.

"I'm trying to break into professional wrestling and no one's done *The Garbage Man.* You've got *The Undertaker* and *Ice Man* but no *Garbage Man,* so I took it." When he finished talking he returned to his paper.

"I don't..." from Fenton.

Roscoe glared at him and said, "You wished. I'm here. End of story."

"You're a wish..." from Fenton.

"Wizard," The Garbage Man finished for him.

"But you wrestle," Fenton was having trouble getting the conversation back on track. He needed help dancing not wrestling.

"That's what a wrestler does Fenton, he wrestles." He couldn't understand why Fenton was having so much trouble with something so obvious. "If I sold shoes I'd be a shoe salesman. Do you see how this naming thing works?"

"I don't need wrestling help. I'm going to a dance on Monday and..." Fenton paused reluctant to admit, "I don't know how."

"There's not that much difference between dancing and wrestling." Roscoe was doing deep knee bends while he talked. "Except for the head butts and body slams they're pretty much the same. You have to be light on your feet and anticipate your opponent's next move." Thinking about wrestling this way moved it up a notch in Fenton's opinion

"Stand up," Roscoe said as he lifted Fenton from the sofa. "Spread your feet the width of your shoulders, bend your knees slightly, and raise up on your toes." He circled Fenton making adjustments as he went. "I'm going to go through the warm up routine I use before a match so do what I do. Okay?"

Fenton nodded cautiously, not sure what *The Garbage Man* had in mind.

"*Day O,*" Roscoe sang while he moved two steps to the left in the same semi-crouched position Fenton was in. "*Da-a-a-O.*" He moved back to the right. "*Daylight comes and I wan go home.*" Fenton followed, taking two steps to the left and one back as they worked their way around the family room. Occasionally Roscoe threw in a dip or a slide as he moved to the rhythm of *The Banana Boat Song.*

They practiced fast numbers and slow ones. "The two step," Roscoe said as he checked Fenton's posture, "is the only move you'll ever need."

After dancing for what felt to Fenton like hours, he held up his hands and said he needed to rest. "No problem," Roscoe answered as he slipped into a faster version of his workout.

Fenton sat on the sofa and closed his eyes.

His mother leaned in the room and said, "While we're out we'll pick up your flowers."

He expected her to say, "Aren't you going to introduce your friend?" but when he opened his eyes, he discovered

The Garbage Man was gone. They only thing to suggest he'd been there was the lingering aroma of garbage and a piece of paper that had fallen under the footstool. When he was sure his mother was gone he picked it up and read, *"You want a piece of me?"*

"If they'd told me this was the day for the third grade dance I would have washed the bus." Mr. Fleener said to each passenger wearing a dress or suit as they climbed aboard. He rubbed his chin and said, "I don't think this old bus has ever carried a prettier load of girls and boys." Fenton made a mental note to ask his mother if he said the same thing to her class. "Tell you what, I might as well turn in my keys," he said as he pulled into the school parking lot, "because I'll never have a better looking group of passengers."

He stood by the door and helped the girls take the step from the bus to the ground. "You don't want a twisted ankle or skinned knee to keep you from dancing."

After lunch, they had a spelling test with words like refreshment, corsage, and suit (not suite).

Then it was time for the dance.

The girls lined up on one side of the gym and the boys on the other. At exactly 2:00 o'clock, Mrs. Brubaker welcomed them to the 25th Third Grade Dance. "Boys check the number you were given and find your partner."

There was no movement on the boy's side. The girls looked at each other and giggled.

"Mrs. Thompson called this morning and said Mary Jane wasn't feeling well." Mrs. Brubaker explained. The students wondered what that had to do with anything. "So, we're one girl short." She waited for the arithmetic to kick in and the boys to figure out what she meant. "Or would be if I hadn't volunteered to take Mary Jane's place." The answer to why she was telling them about Mrs. Thompson's call and what she was doing about it hit them all at the same time; one of the boys was going to be her partner.

The line broke and the boys fell over each other getting to the girls side of the gym to find out who had the same number as theirs.

One by one couples paired off. Fenton and Billy Gilsky were still looking, checking numbers to make sure the girls who'd been taken hadn't made a mistake.

Dorthea Simmons stepped away from the gym wall. "Fifteen?" Billy asked pleading for her to have his number. She shook her head no. A look of panic swept across his face and his shoulder's sagged when he realized he would be Mrs. Brubaker's partner.

Fenton watched hopelessly as couples exchanged wrist corsages and boutonnieres. "Twenty-two?" he asked one of the girls and rather than answer, she nodded to Dorthea.

"Are you looking for twenty-two?" Dorthea asked, having learned from Sally Graves two weeks before that Fenton would be her partner. She held up the slip of paper with her number on it.

"Well, yeah, I guess…" Fenton stammered as Dorthea took the corsage from him and slipped it on her wrist. "That is, I think…" he mumbled as she pinned a boutonniere to the lapel of his sport coat. "Gee whiz, I mean…" Fenton looked around to see what the other couples were doing.

"Form a circle around me. Hold your partners hand so you don't lose one another," Mrs. Brubaker's announcement was met by nervous laughter from the students. "Our disc jockey,

Ms Chalmer, is going to play songs from my collection of records from the '50's." She heard murmurs as the students tried to figure out what she meant by the 50's. "Did she have 50 records?" someone wondered. "Did each one last 50 minutes?" Another asked what a record was.

"Keep your eyes on me as she plays the first song. If you know the two step you can start dancing. If you don't, watch and learn." Mrs. Brubaker got ready to dance; feet apart the width of her shoulders, knees slightly bent, and her heels raised an inch off the floor. "Hit it Ms C!" she hollered over the excited voices of the children.

"Day O," the voice of Harry Belafonte echoed through the gym. Students looked at each other trying to figure out if it was a song or some kind of joke. They watched Mrs. Brubaker take two steps to her left. *"Da-a-a-O,"* Harry Belafonte sang as she moved back to the right. ***"Daylight comes and I wan go home."*** She took two steps to the left.

No one moved, afraid of looking foolish in front of the others. The buzz of voices rose as Fenton broke from the circle and walked confidently toward Mrs. Brubaker. She smiled, took his right hand in hers, and placed her other hand on his shoulder.

"Six foot, seven foot, eight foot hut." Harry Belafonte continued as Mrs. Brubaker and Fenton circled the floor, caught up in the simple rhythm of the song.

Encouraged by Ms Chalmer, others joined them trying to imitate their steps. Boys could be heard saying, "If Tug can do it so can I." When the song finished, Mrs. Brubaker curtsied, Fenton bowed and walked back to Dorthea.

"Now let's see how you do with *Rock Around The Clock*," Mrs. Brubaker announced and looked for Billy Gilsky as the dancers tried to keep up with the music of Bill Haley and the Comets.

"I can't believe you like to dance," Dorthea said, "most boys don't."

"Well," Fenton said as he took two steps to the left, barely missing her toe, "I guess you could say people have only seen a piece of me." He chuckled after he said it, sure she had no idea what he was talking about.

"Are you going to the dance at the Community Center?" A girl asked Fenton as she sailed by. "He has to be the best boy dancer in school," she told her partner.

"Last dance boys and girls then it's time to go," Mrs. Brubaker clapped her hands and announced as she dabbed a handkerchief at the perspiration on her forehead. Later, as she and Ms. Chalmer were cleaning up, they discussed this years dance and agreed it was the best one ever.

"See the pyramids along the Nile," the voice of Patti Page poured from the speakers and blended with the dancers who two hours before were dreading the experience, but now wished it could last a little longer.

Finally, the strains of *You Belong To Me,* stopped echoing through the gym and silence followed. Reluctantly partners separated and headed for the bus. Dorthea leaned forward, kissed Fenton lightly on the cheek, and walked out of the gym.

He stood motionless at the top of the free throw circle. His cheek burned where her lips touched it. His legs were wobbly and he was afraid if he moved he'd wake up and discover it had all been a dream.

He was pulled from his reverie by the sound of a mop sliding across the floor. Fenton turned and saw a large man in green coveralls and work boots walking toward him.

"Garbage Man?" Fenton called to him. "Is that you? I thought you'd be wrestling somewhere."

"The Garbage Man thing didn't work out. I smelled so bad no one wanted to get close enough to wrestle so I changed to *The Custodian*. He pointed to a corner of the gym and hollered, **"Hey kid, get off the floor with your street shoes!"** He looked back at Fenton, smiled, and asked, "What do you think?"

Fenton didn't answer. Something *The Custodian* said about getting off the gym floor got his attention. Then it hit him. "Hey Dorthea," he called as he ran after her, "can I sit with you on the bus?"

Chapter 11
THE DAY THE EARTH STOOD STILL

It took awhile for Fenton Alowishus Tug to figure out what was going on.

He got on the school bus the way he usually did; the hood of his sweatshirt pulled over his head, hands thrust in the pockets of his jeans, and his backpack slung over his shoulder. He looked like every boy who got on the bus.

He walked halfway down the aisle, lowered his backpack, and was about to sit down when he realized someone was in his seat. If it had been a guy, he would have bumped him with his knee and told him to move over. It wasn't a guy, it was a girl, sitting in the seat he'd occupied since the first day of school.

"Can't go 'til everyone's seated," Mr. Fleener hollered over his shoulder. Billy Gilsky waved, letting Fenton know there was an open place next to him.

Sitting at the back of the bus presented a problem.

Every boy knew if they didn't have to wait at bus stops, if Mr. Fleener was able to make it to school without stopping for a red light or a stalled car, and if he parked in front of the other busses instead of behind them, there would be enough time to get in a full inning of kickball before school started.

This morning, other than losing time because someone was sitting in his seat, everything was working the way it was supposed to. As the bus pulled into the number one spot, the boys grabbed their backpacks, and leaned forward, ready to dash to the front the moment the door opened.

That's when Fenton figured out what was going on but by then it was too late to do anything about it.

The instant Mr. Fleener reached for the lever that opened the door, the girls stood and stepped in the aisle, blocking the way.

Mr. Fleener, used to the stampede of boys trying to be the first off the bus and not hearing it, looked at the girl beside his seat and asked, "Something wrong?"

She shook her head and said, "I want to thank you for getting us to school safely this morning." When she finished, she stepped off the bus and another girl took her place. She complimented him on the smooth starts as he pulled away from the bus stops. When she left another said she admired the way he used his mirrors to see what was happening behind him. She was followed by someone who appreciated the cleanliness of the bus.

And so it went until the last girl thanked him for parking close to the curb.

The problem was, each compliment delivered to Mr. Fleener took time off the clock and when the last girl stepped onto the parking lot, the boys had to run to get to class on time. Forget about kickball. Forget about standing in the dugout and shooting the breeze while waiting for your turn at the plate. They knew Ms Chalmer was standing by the door to her room, ready to close it the moment the bell stopped ringing.

What Fenton didn't realize was the scene on the bus was just the tip of the iceberg.

At recess, Ms Chalmer said it was the girls turn to leave first and by the time the boys arrived at the playground, they were on it, throwing the ball to one another.

Rudy "Big Foot" Griggs stepped on the field and said, "Play time's over girls, we're here now." He was surprised when they continued playing like they hadn't heard him.

"Hey," he hollered, "are you deaf? **Get! Off! My! Field!**" It was obvious he was upset; his face was red and his hands were balled into fists.

A girl rolling the ball to the catcher stopped and strolled confidently toward him. She took her time getting there and if she was worried about taking on the meanest guy in school it didn't show.

That explains it, Fenton thought. The slowdown on the bus. The field occupied by girls. Misty Eindorf was behind this. She was in Mrs. Brubaker's room and by far the best athlete in school.

Fenton had noticed when her back was to him she was wearing a tee shirt with the outline of a truck. He could see the *Eindorf Used Trucks and Cars* printed beneath the picture. He couldn't see the part that said, *"Come on down, it doesn't cost anything to talk,"* because it was tucked into her jeans.

Now with her facing him, he saw, "**G.A.P.**" stenciled on the front and beneath it, "**Girls At Play.**"

Misty put her hands on her hips, leaned toward Rudy and said, "I don't see your name on the field!"

"That's because you're a girl and girls can't read." After he said it, Rudy knelt down and wrote, "Rudys Field," in the dirt. When he finished he stood and glared at her, daring her to top that.

She smiled as she erased the line from one side of the d and drew it on the other side with the toe of her shoe. It now read, "Rubys Field." She glared at him and told him to, "Read it and weep Flat Foot."

Things were moving too fast for Rudy. He thought putting his name on the field was pretty clever but when she changed Rudy to Ruby, he realized he was in over his head. He was going to need a heavy hitter on this one. The situation called for a quick thinker. "Get Perky," he growled and immediately two boys took off for the outfield where they knew they'd find Perky Bergbinder the 3rd sitting at the picnic table, reading a book.

They returned, dragging a reluctant Perky with them. He pushed his glasses in place and asked, "What's going on?"

"That," Rudy said and pointed to the name in the dirt.

"Well," Perky said in his usual high pitched nasal voice, "you're missing an apostrophe." He pointed to the place between they y and s in Rubys. When no one moved to change it, he reached down, added the mark, and started to leave.

Rudy grabbed the back of his shirt and said, "Stick around, I may need you."

"Hi Perky." Misty said as she batted her eyes and smiled.

Perky blushed. He fiddled with the pencils in his pocket protector and said, "Hi Misty." In the confusion of being brought to the field and finding the punctuation error, he hadn't noticed her. He was surprised she knew his name.

"We're losing valuable game time. Why don't you and your little friends go jump rope, play with dolls, or whatever you do at recess." When he finished, Rudy started to step onto the field when Misty, without breaking eye contact said, "Ruby!"

Ruby Durham hurried across the infield and Misty told her to, "Show Two Foot the proclamation."

Ruby reached in her purse but stopped when she heard Billy Gilsky laugh and tell Brian Alexander, "You can't play kickball and carry a purse."

She ignored his comment and produced a folded piece of paper. She opened it and read, "To all those present greetings. I am pleased to announce today, April 23rd, 2008, is *Girl's Day* at Buffalo Bill Cody Elementary." She pointed to the bottom of the page and said, "It's signed by Principal Logan."

Rudy grabbed the paper and turned it over. "You didn't read the back where he said he was kidding, he meant to say it was boy's day."

"Monkey see. Monkey do." Misty shot back.

"Are you calling me a monkey?" Rudy asked and took a menacing step toward her.

"You don't have to call a monkey, you peel a banana and he shows up."

"Is there a problem?" Ms Chalmer asked as she left her seat in the bleachers and stepped between them.

"Nope," from Misty.

"Not that I'm aware of," Rudy added.

"If there isn't a problem, why aren't you playing?" Ms Chalmer looked at Misty then Rudy.

"We were, ah…" Rudy tried but couldn't come up with an answer.

"Choosing sides." Misty finished for him.

"Yeah, seeing who kicks first. That kind of thing." Rudy added. He had to admit, he appreciated that Misty didn't start bawling about how unfair the boys were.

"Girls against the boys?" Misty said and waved for the girls to take the field.

"Seriously?" Rudy said through a laugh. "What are you going to do for the rest of recess, pout because we beat you so bad?"

"We won't be the ones pouting Slew Foot. Think what the other kids will say when they hear you were beaten by a bunch of girls."

"Not going to happen."

"Watch us."

"Recess is over, everyone inside." Ms Chalmer announced and started up the path to the school building. She stopped, looked back, and saw Misty and Rudy facing each other, neither willing to be the first to leave.

In the lunchroom, the third grade girls were bunched around Misty. She was holding a piece of notebook paper with the drawing of a kickball field, giving a crash course in how to play.

The boys at the next table laughed when they heard Dorthea Simmons ask, "Which one is first base? They look the same to me." They could hardly wait for afternoon recess. The problem as they saw it was, do you get it over with quickly or drag it out and prolong the agony.

Looking back, Fenton could see, that was the moment things began to unravel for the boys kickball team.

Rudy "Big Foot" Griggs, still upset over being outsmarted by Misty, lifted a dill pickle off his plate, and flicked it towards the girls table. They screamed, the boys laughed, and Rudy felt the hand of Mrs. Granger, the cafeteria monitor, on his shoulder. She'd seen the whole thing, jerked her head and said, "Follow me Rudy, let's see how funny Principal Logan thinks you are." Rudy said he was just joking around but Mrs. Granger told him to, "Save it for the judge."

Billy Gilsky and Brian Alexander were surprised when Ms Chalmer lifted the geography book they were sharing and saw a list of names on a piece of paper. With Rudy out of the picture, they were trying to come up with the best lineup for the game. The boy's team would be short two more players because they'd be spending their recess at the chalk board finishing the sentence, "The thing I like about geography is…"

One by one the team decreased in size. A seldom used player, when he heard he was in the starting lineup for the afternoon game, got sick to his stomach and spent the afternoon in the nurse's office. Another was talking in line on the way to an assembly. A third punched his friend on the arm and was sent to the school secretary to watch a video on bullying.

On his way to the playground Fenton whispered, "I wish I knew how this is going to end."

He heard the sound of a motor scooter behind him. The horn beeped as the driver wove between students walking to the field. He paused a moment when he got to Fenton then continued to the playground. He wore a leather jacket, plastic helmet, and goggles. As the scooter sped away Fenton saw *W. W. Inc. Messenger Service*, printed across the back of the driver's jacket.

For the first time that day, Fenton saw a ray of hope. His wish had been heard. Yes there'd been some surprises, and yes they boy's team had experienced setbacks, but with the help of *W.W. Inc.* they were home free.

Word of the game spread through school and after a quick meeting in the teachers lounge, it was decided they would all have recess at the same time so the students could watch. Some teachers took advantage of the situation and worked the game into their lesson plan. Mr. Dice saw it as a way to demonstrate the principle of action-reaction by having the kids in his room drop a kickball from a window and calculate how high it bounced after it hit the ground.

In the first grade, arithmetic problems were formed around totaling scores inning by inning.

"Do children in Africa play kickball?" Mrs. Kramer asked and had her fourth grade students to find Botswana on a map.

When Fenton arrived at the field, he saw the scooter balanced on a kick stand and the rider, walking through the crowd, calling his name. Fenton waved to get his attention.

The messenger pushed his goggles up on his forehead and nodded when he saw Fenton's hand. "Fenton Tug?" he asked when he got close enough for Fenton to hear. "Sign for this," the messenger said as he reached in a worn canvas bag and pulled out an envelope.

After Fenton signed, the messenger waited for a tip. When he didn't see Fenton stick his hands in his pockets looking for loose change, he pulled down his goggles, climbed on the scooter, and drove off.

Fenton hesitantly opened the telegram. It was from someone named J. Brandon Yarlboro, Dispatch Manager at Wish Wizard, Inc.

"To whom it may concern. In a meeting on March 3rd, 2008 and covered by a memo of the same date sent to Wish Wizard Inc., Ken Flounder of Flounder Wealth Management, and Fenton Alowishus Tug. The purpose of the memo is to inform all parties that the following decision was made by the W.W. Inc. steering committee. To act in a responsible manner, encourage fair play, and provide an equal opportunity for all players regardless of gender, this organization will remain neutral on the girls versus boys kickball issue."

It was signed by J. Brandon Yarlboro and said he looked forward to working together in the future on less sensitive matters. Below his signature he'd written, *"Have a nice day."*

Fenton folded the message and stuck it in his pocket. He glanced in the dugout to see who was on his team. The only person there was Perky Bergbinder chewing on a carrot stick and reading a book on *Kickball Fundamentals* written by Coach Peewee Barnett.

"Hey Tug, you going to kick or are you ought here to work on your suntan?" Misty hollered and Fenton responded by walking to home plate like a condemned man on his way to the gallows. When he got there, he didn't go through his usual routine; tap the plate with his right foot and tug on the cuff of his jeans. Instead he took two steps back and hollered with little enthusiasm, "Slow and smooth."

He was surprised when Misty answered with, "Sorry Tug. It's *Pot Luck Day*, you take what you get."

Fenton was stunned. There were rules on how kickball was played and Misty was breaking all of them. The pitcher never argued with the kicker and in his years of playing kickball he'd never heard of *Pot Luck Day.*" While Fenton recovered from her comment Perky read out loud, *"Pot Luck Day. A seldom used strategy intended to throw off the opponent. The pitcher can select from an endless variety of pitches."* When he finished he held up Peewee Barnett's book. Fenton thought if Misty used *Pot Luck Day* to throw him off his game, it worked.

To make matters worse, she rolled the ball with her hand on top, not underneath like everyone else. "No. No." Fenton wanted to tell her, "Your doing it all wrong. Your hand goes..." He watched the ball roll toward him but before he could kick, it stopped three feet from the plate and spun back towards the pitcher's mound.

Misty laughed at the surprised look on Fenton's face. "Never heard of backspin? Well hold on to your hat Tuggie because here comes the sidewinder." She leaned forward, drew back her arm, and prepared to roll a ball that would start toward third base then shoot toward home the instant it touched the ground. Before she released the ball, Dorthea Simmons yelled, "Stop!" She was standing on first base because Misty had told her it didn't make any difference where she stood, no one would get that far.

Dorthea had watched Fenton walk to the plate, heard Misty yell at him, and made him look foolish by the way she rolled the ball. She'd closed her eyes and remembered Fenton at the third grade dance. He was the only boy to volunteer to dance with Mrs. Brubaker. He'd given her a corsage and turned out to be a wonderful dancer. He'd stopped several times to ask if she wanted a cup of punch or to rest before the next dance. When the dance ended and the other couples split up, he sat beside her on the bus.

Misty called for a time out and walked to first base. "You got a problem? It's time to close the deal. We've got him right where we want him."

Dorthea shook her head. "We don't have him where we want him Misty, you do." After saying it she sat on the base and tugged at her shoestrings. "It doesn't mean anything if were not playing their best."

Misty disagreed. "A win is a win." She repeated a phrase she'd heard her father say after selling a van with a faulty transmission to a family with four kids under the age of six. When she saw Dorthea wasn't going to change her mind, she looked around to see who she could get to replace her. She saw the left and center fielders sitting on the ground. They were teammates with Perky on the *Math-A-Maniacs* and decided if he kicked the ball to them, they wouldn't catch it.

"Okay," Misty said as she threw her hands in the air and walked back to the mound. "Game over," she hollered, kicked the ball into the bleachers, and walked angrily off the field.

Fenton remained behind when everyone started up the path to school. He was trying to figure out what was going on. There was no way he and Perky could have won a game against the girls team with or without Misty Eindorf playing for them. There was too much field for the two of them to cover and this was Perky's first game. He was surprised to find out there was a book about kickball, he thought you learned how to play from other kids.

His thoughts were brought back to the moment when Dorthea asked, "You want to walk to school together?" He shrugged it was okay with him. He was anxious to find out what she said to Misty, he'd been too far away to hear.

Long after everyone left the field, Perky sat in the dugout trying to memorize the odd list of words in the back of *Kickball Fundamentals* under the heading, "Common Kickball Terms." Squeeze play, bunt, and foul ball were part of a two page list. When he realized everyone was gone, he tucked the book under his arm and started up the path to school.

He was halfway there when a man wearing a helmet and goggles pulled his motor scooter along side him and asked, "Want a lift?"

Perky nodded he did and climbed on.

"Quite a game wasn't it?" the stranger said.

"Is it over?" Perky had been so engrossed in reading about kickball he'd missed his chance to play.

"For today but there'll be another game tomorrow." The driver said when they reached the entrance to the school.

Perky was sure the driver was right about tomorrow's game but equally sure he wouldn't be playing. Given the choice he preferred staying inside, working arithmetic problems with the *Math-A-Maniacs*. There were fewer personality issues and the answers more predictable.

Chapter 12
Rong Address

Edgar Tug, Fenton Tug's father, entered the hall from the garage, hung his cap on a hook in the closet, hollered "Honey, I'm home," to Mrs. Tug, and picked up the stack of mail from the table by the front door. As he worked his way through the half dozen envelopes in his hand he quietly muttered, "Bill. Bill. Another bill."

He stopped and studied one more closely than the others. "Fenton!" he called up the stairway to the second floor then hollered again, waiting for the bedroom door to open and Fenton to come bounding down the stairs.

He was about to call a third time when Fenton stepped out of the kitchen with milk on his upper lip and cookie crumbs clinging to the corners of his mouth. "You looking for me?"

"Yes Fenton, I am." There was a note of irritation in his father's voice. He held the up the letters and asked, "What am I holding in my hand?"

Fenton wasn't sure which hand he was talking about. He'd fallen for the, "What am I holding in my hand?" trick at school and been laughed at because he'd looked at the hand Brian Alexander held in front of him, not the one behind his back. His father wouldn't pull something like that would he? "Letters?" he said cautiously, thinking if I'm wrong I'll say it was a guess, not my real answer.

"Indeed," his father said as he shuffled the letters. "I want to read something to you, okay?"

Fenton thought about the question then shook his head yes, it was fine with him.

His father held up an envelope and read, "Mr. Edgar Tug." He looked at Fenton and raised his eyebrows.

"Okay," Fenton said cautiously after looking for hidden traps or trouble areas and not finding any.

His father continued. "12435 Gator Way." When he finished he moved the first envelope to the bottom of the stack and held up a second one. "Again, this is addressed to, Mr. Edgar Tug." This time after he said it he pointed to the envelope and then to himself indicating he was the one the letter was addressed to.

Fenton listened, not sure where this was going.

"12435 Gator Way," his father looked at Fenton over the top of his glasses to make sure he was paying attention.

Fenton nodded he was.

He held up a third envelope but instead of saying, "Mr. Edgar Tug," he said, "Mrs. Gloria Stuffelbeam." Fenton started to say hold on a minute, there must be a mistake, but before he could his father finished with, "12435 **Lobo** Way."

"Now Fenton, let me ask you a question. Have you seen Mrs. Gloria Stuffelbeam in this house?"

Fenton shook his head no.

"Is this 12435 Lobo Way?"

Fenton shook his head no.

"So, what do you make of the obvious difference between this letter and the others?" His father held the one to Mrs. Stuffelbeam in his left hand and those addressed to him in his right. He leaned toward Fenton and asked, "What is your conclusion?"

"I conclude…" Fenton had no idea what his father was talking about or what he was supposed to say. "That is, I think…" He looked around hoping his mother would step in the hallway and say they should wash their hands because dinner would be ready in five minutes.

"This is not rocket science Fenton. It's not a question on that AST test or whichever one they take in high school is called." His statement was followed by an awkward silence as Fenton studied the rug, hoping an answer would appear in the loops and swirls of its pattern.

"It was delivered to the wrong house!" His father said slowly, exasperated that his youngest son, currently a third grade student at Buffalo Bill Cody Elementary, couldn't answer a simple question involving the U.S. Postal Service. "The letter that was supposed to go to Mrs. Stuffelbeam was delivered to our house by mistake."

"Well sure there's that but I thought you meant…" Fenton told himself to stop talking, to not say another word, and the problem with today's mail will blow over and be forgotten.

"Suppose it's twenty years in the future." His father changed the tone of his voice. He no longer sounded angry but more like a friend asking a question at the school lunch table. "And, you are the father of two boys."

"Two boys?" Fenton gasped.

"And they take turns bringing in the mail."

Fenton's shoulders dropped. He hoped this wasn't going to be a question about two brothers going to get the mail. One leaves Chicago at three in the afternoon and the other leaves Los Angeles an hour later and he has to figure out which one gets to the mail box first.

His father continued. "Among the letters your son brings in you find one that has been delivered to the wrong address."

Fenton was confused. He wondered if he'd missed something important while he was thinking about his sons racing across the country to get the mail. "Was it the older or younger one's turn to bring in the mail." Talking about one being older and the other younger seemed impersonal to him. If they were his sons he'd call them by their names. He couldn't imagine sitting at the dinner table and saying, "Older son, pass the creamed peas."

"It doesn't make any difference which one gets the mail. But, if it helps you picture what's going on, let's say its the youngest."

"What's his name?" Fenton was sure he'd get the boys mixed up if he didn't know who they were.

"It's not important but, for your sake, let's say it's Fenton Tug Jr."

Fenton shook his head. "I'd never name him that." He couldn't imagine what it would be like to go through life being called Junior. He shuddered when he pictured Lester Banks Jr. sitting alone at a lunch table.

His father waved his hands. "Forget about names. Forget which brother brought in the mail. Or whether it's Tuesday or Thursday. Just listen to the story and answer the question. Okay?"

Fenton shrugged.

"So, your youngest son is holding an envelope delivered to the wrong address, he doesn't know what to do, and turns to you for guidance." His father motioned he could answer at any time.

"I'd tell him…" Fenton wasn't sure what to say. It seemed to him there were more important things to talk with his son about than a letter delivered to the wrong address. He would ask about his day at school and tell him what to do if someone in his class named Brian Alexander took his arithmetic assignment and threw it out the school bus window. He wasn't sure what he'd tell him to do with the letter. "I think he should…"

"Write, *Wrong Address,* on the envelope and put it in the mail box for heaven's sake." His father threw his hands in the air, exasperated by their conversation and Fenton's inability to answer a simple question. It bothered him to watch his lips move as he counted on his fingers and pulled on the bottom of his sweater hoping something would pop in his mind.

"So?" Fenton's father held up the Stufflebeam letter.

Fenton studied it, not sure what his father wanted him to do or say. He was still reeling from the thought of having two sons. He tried to imagine coming home from work, hanging his hat on a peg in the closet, and picking the mail from the table like his father did. He wondered what kind of job he had and when he hollered, "Honey I'm home," who would answer. He hoped it wasn't Melissa Treadwell, the girl who sat across from him on the school bus and stuck out her tongue when he looked at her.

He realized while he'd been thinking about his family, his father had placed the envelope in his hand and said something before finishing with, "…and, put it in the mailbox." Fenton hated to tell him he'd missed part of what he said.

He looked at the envelope then back at his father who'd turned and was walking away. He wanted to call to him and ask what he said before he got to the part about putting it in the mailbox.

He replayed their conversation but couldn't get past wondering what his family was doing without him there to help answer complicated questions like what to do with a letter delivered to their house by mistake.

He studied the name on the envelope and remembered what his father said. He found a pencil and carefully wrote, "Rong Address," above the name of Mrs. Gloria Stuffelbeam. He drew a line from the end of his note to the address and put an arrow on the end of the line.

He walked across the street and slid the letter in the slot on top of the mail box. "That takes care of that," he told himself and walked victoriously back to his house.

The next day he was in his room carefully placing dominos on end, creating a line that curved across the floor and looped around a leg of his bed when he heard his father call his name.

He went to the door and listened, hoping he'd called his brother's name.

His father called again and this time he was sure it was his name. He walked down stairs and saw his father standing beside the table holding a letter in his hand.

He relaxed. He was off the hook. He was home free. It was his brother's day to get the mail, not his. He couldn't possibly be blamed for putting the letters on the wrong side of the table or stacking them upside down.

His father pushed an envelope toward him and said, "For you," before turning his attention to the rest of the mail.

He picked up something else from his father; a frown, a shake of the head, a look of disappointment. He thought he heard him mutter something about why he couldn't be more like his brother but he wasn't sure.

He looked at the letter. It was the one to Mrs. Gloria Stuffelbeam he'd put in the mailbox yesterday afternoon. He looked at his father then back at the envelope. He started to ask why he'd given it to him when he saw a circle around the word, "Rong," and an arrow pointing to the side where, "Wrong," was written in large print and the W underlined.

It took him a moment to figure out what was going on. That can't be right, he said to himself, then looked at his father and said, "That can't be right." He pointed to the arrow and the word wrong. "Isn't rong right and wrong rong?"

"No son, I'm afraid he got you on that one. Wrong is right and rong is wrong. At least it was the last time I looked."

Fenton waited, not sure what to do. Rong being wrong didn't make sense; they sounded the same if you said them quickly. He went to his room and pulled the dictionary from the bookshelf next to his desk. He made his way to the r's then the ro's. He let his finger slide down the page to rondure, rood, roof, but he could find no rong.

He had to admit the mailman was right. He carefully put a W in front of Rong, spelling the word correctly but it looked funny to him.

He went downstairs, crossed the street, and dropped the envelope in the mailbox hoping the letter was no longer his problem.

When he walked in his room the next afternoon, he saw the Stuffelbeam letter sitting on top of his desk. Beneath. "WRong Address," was a new note. *"Address is Correct. Mrs. Gloria Stuffelbeam lives at 12435 Lobo Way."*

He stared at the envelope, baffled by the note. Somewhere along the line things had taken a wrong turn. The point of the note he'd written was to let the postman know he'd delivered the letter to the wrong address. He'd never intended to say Mrs. Gloria Stuffelbeam lived at his house.

He went downstairs for supper. He wanted to ask his father about the returned envelope but knew the minute he did he'd start talking about his sons, twenty years from now, facing the letter delivered to the wrong address question and he didn't want to go there right now.

When he got back to his room the envelope was laying exactly where he left it. He went to the window and looked at the swing set in the backyard. He walked to his closet and moved his clothes from one end of the pole to the other. He fiddled with the radio trying to find a station playing the kind of music he liked. Finally he sat down at his desk and wrote beneath the mailman's note, "This is 12435 Gator Way. Mrs. Gloria Stuffelbeam does not live here." He studied the note, removed the period after the last word, and replaced it with an exclamation point. He drew a line under it so now it read, *"Mrs. Gloria Stuffelbeam does not live here!"*

Feeling satisfied with what he'd written, he took the letter to the mailbox. He reread his note and could find no punctuation errors or misspelled words, nothing that could possibly be misunderstood by even the newest, most inexperienced postal employee. He was sure his note would bring an end to the problem and get the material in the envelope to the proper person.

"How's the situation with the you know what coming along?" his father asked when walked back in the house.

"Good," Fenton replied not sure which situation he was talking about. The fact that Rudy "Big Foot" Griggs the school bully had taken his lunch money for the third day in a row. That his friend Myron Cleeg told him his parents were thinking of moving. Or that Brian Alexander took his home work assignment so now he had to work all the problems at the end of Chapter Six instead of just four Ms Chalmer assigned.

He especially didn't want to go into the details of the note he'd received from the postman.

"Your writing was clear and legible?" his father asked.

Fenton nodded yes.

"No chance what you've written can be misunderstood?"

Fenton shook his head no.

"Well then," his father said with a note of satisfaction, "that should just about wrap up the Stuffelbeam problem shouldn't it?"

Fenton shrugged he hoped so.

When he came to supper the next evening he was surprised to find the Stuffelbeam letter laying on his plate. The note he'd underlined and ended with an exclamation point was circled and a line attached to it, went over the top of the envelope and part way down the back. "See address on front of envelope for proper location of Mrs. Gloria Stuffelbeam. If," the postman had underlined the word if, "she lived at your house the address would be 12435 Gator Way!!" The double exclamation point at the end of the note did not escape Fenton's attention.

He looked up and saw his father watching him. His brother sat with his fork and spoon in his hand, waiting for his father to say it was okay to start eating.

"Is there a problem?" his father asked.

"No sir. I mean, well, yes sir. I thought I had..." Fenton didn't know what to say. He wondered why it couldn't have been his brothers turn to get the mail the day the Stuffelbeam letter arrived. He wondered what his sons would think of a father who couldn't handle a simple mail delivery problem.

"Ah, the infamous Stuffelbeam letter." There was a touch of disappointment in his father's voice that the problem hadn't been taken care of by now. "It looks like Bill Alexander is having some fun at your expense."

"Who?" Something clicked in Fenton's mind when he heard the postman's name.

"Our mailman, Bill Alexander," his father answered as he spread a pat of butter on his dinner roll. "I think his son goes to your school. Bob, or Ben, I'm not sure what his name is."

"Brian? Brian Alexander?" Fenton said almost automatically. That explains everything he thought. The old saying of like father like son seemed to be working in the Alexander family. Or maybe it was the equally old saying of the apple not falling far from the tree. Fenton wasn't sure which described the situation best but at the mention of Bill Alexander's name things fell in place.

"May I be excused?" Fenton asked as he picked up his plate and carried it to the sink.

"He just picked at his food," his mother whispered to his father.

"He's upset about the Stufflebeam letter," his father told her.

His brother Felix slid Fenton's Jell-O salad closer to his plate.

When Fenton got to his room he put the letter on his desk and walked to his bed. He came back to his desk, sat down, put his head in his hands and mumbled, "I wish I knew what to do."

The doorbell rang.

He ignored it and studied the front of the envelope.

The doorbell rang.

He stepped in the hallway and hollered, "Someone's at the door!" He heard voices coming from the dining room but nothing to suggest one of them was going to see who was there.

The doorbell rang.

He went downstairs, peeked through the small window next to the door, and saw a man wearing a worn leather jacket and stocking cap standing on the porch, checking the address against a paper in his hand.

Fenton opened the door and asked, "Can I help you?"

The stranger took a step toward him and announced, "Taxi's here." He held up the piece of paper he'd received before being dispatched to Fenton's house. "Tug?" He pointed to a name at the top of the paper.

Fenton was confused. Nothing had been said at supper about calling a cab but then he'd left after the food was served. "My father must have..." He stopped when the taxi driver shook his head and held up the paper so Fenton could read it. "I don't think so unless," he mumbled as he studied the paper a second time, "his name's Fenton." The driver paced nervously back and forth as he considered the implications of an additional passenger. "I was expecting a kid, nothing was said about an adult. I guess it's okay but that means when I'm finished I have to go back to headquarters and fill out..."

While the taxi driver was talking, Fenton studied the name tag clipped to his jacket. "Hsiw Drawziw," he read and tried to sound it out but even saying it slowly, it didn't make sense.

The taxi driver looked over his shoulder to make sure no one was listening and whispered, "Backwards."

"I'm sorry?" His comment took Fenton by surprise. Was he saying just because he had trouble reading his name he was a slow learner? Or that he'd driven to Fenton's house backwards?"

"Read. It. Backwards." The driver said through clenched teeth, his lips barely moving. When he finished he tapped the name tag with his finger and winked.

This was something Fenton had trouble doing. Most of the time he could sound words out if the weren't too long and were going in the right direction. But if they were printed backwards he didn't know where to start.

The driver pointed to the w in Hsiw.

Okay, Fenton nodded.

He moved to the next letter when he was sure Fenton got the first one.

"Wish?" Fenton said. The driver smiled and would have given him an encouraging pat on the back if the screen door hadn't been in the way

When he started on the second word Fenton saw it immediately. "Wizard. You're a Wish Wizard?"

"Shhh. Not so loud," the driver hissed and placed a finger against his lips telling Fenton to quiet down.

"Why are you here?" Fenton whispered.

The driver looked confused. He studied the paper thinking it explained everything. "Something about delivering a letter to," the driver studied the paper and Fenton saw him trying to figure out how to pronounce Stuffelbeam. Finally, he pointed to the name and said, "Her."

"Oh that," Fenton said in a way that suggested he didn't like being reminded of the letter he'd struggled with all week.

"I'm supposed to give you this," the driver said as he slipped the Stufflebeam letter from a pocket of his jacket. Fenton could have sworn it was still on the desk in his room. Then he remembered his wish and shrugged. "I guess I thought they'd send someone, I don't know, more familiar with postal activities."

"They could have. Yes. Absolutely." The driver nodded as he thought about what Fenton said. His face brightened. "Unless," he looked at Fenton and smiled, "they thought… you could…deliver it yourself and…I could…"

"Take me?"

"There."

"To?"

"Her." The taxi driver pointed to the name on the envelope.

"In?"

"That," he said and nodded to a late model car parked at the curb. Fenton saw "Hsiw Draziw," written in a circle on the front door. He's was too far away to see it but Fenton was sure the wishbone of a turkey was in the center of the circle.

"When?" Fenton asked hoping the driver would say he wouldn't be available until tomorrow or he couldn't possibly work him in until the weekend?

"Now," he said and when Fenton hesitated, he pointed to the taxi. "Better get a move on, the meter's running."

Fenton hollered toward the dining room that he was going out for a few minutes and ran to catch up with the taxi driver as he hurried down the sidewalk to his car.

They drove the few short blocks to Lobo Way, turned the corner, and continued until they came to 12435.

The driver pulled to the curb and turned off the engine. He removed the envelope from his jacket and handed it to Fenton. "Okay. All you have to do is go to the door, deliver the letter and your troubles are over."

Fenton took the letter and opened the car door. He hoped it would be that easy but doubted it.

"And Fenton," he turned thinking the driver would say, "I've had some experience with this kind of thing, I'll do it for you." Instead he said, "A word to the wise. Don't fool around with Uncle Sam."

Fenton looked at the sidewalk that stretched from the street to the front door of the house. He tried not to think of the terrible things that could happen on a surface like that. Toys, left by someone who'd been playing outside were spread along the path. An occasional crack in the sidewalk allowed tufts of grass to stick through the concrete. A glob of mud, dried and cracked, lay on the front step.

He sighed, stepped out of the car, and walked carefully to the house.

When he reached the porch he started to push the button mounted next to the door but stopped when he saw a note beneath it. He leaned forward, squinted, and tried to read what it said. "**Don't work**," someone had written with a felt tipped pen, and below it he saw what looked like "**Knot,**" or "**Knack**."

He bent his knees and crouched down, hoping to get a closer look at the word. He was about to give up and ask the taxi driver for help when he discovered he was looking in the face of a three year old girl on the other side of the screen door.

"Mommy," she yelled, "some man is wooking in our doow."

Fenton shook his head and stumbled backward. "No, really, I'm not..."

The child's mother appeared holding a tea towel in one hand and a half dried glass in the other. "Yeah?" She said as if expecting Fenton to ask her to subscribe to a magazine or sign up for a lawn care service.

"Yes, well, ah, Mrs. Stuffelbeam, Gloria actually, I have a, this, letter that was…" Fenton stammered and pushed the letter toward the screen door. He started to tell her how it had been delivered to his house by mistake and he'd put it in the mail box but Brian Alexander's father kept giving it back. Before he could, the screen door opened and she yanked the envelope from his hand, pointed to the writing and asked, "You do that?"

"At first…" he started to say but before he could she said, "Weird," and tore it open.

She studied the letter, looked at Fenton and asked, "What's today's date?"

Fenton looked over his shoulder hoping something would jog his memory. He was pretty sure it was Thursday but he had no idea what month it was. "March, I think, or maybe…" he stopped and tried to remember what he'd written in the top right corner of the spelling test he'd taken that afternoon.

"Thought so," she said. "February sale at Dimmelmans. Store wide." She looked at Fenton and finished with, "Too late."

His mother had taken him to Dimmelmans for his first day of school outfit. He was trying to remember what side of town it was on when she opened the screen door, thrust the letter in his hand and said, "No thanks," as she fastened the hook on the screen door and walked away.

The little girl stared at Fenton for a moment then said, "Yeah, no tanks mistewh," and followed her mother back to the kitchen.

He returned to the taxi where the driver, opened the door and asked, "Everything okay?"

He shrugged, his usual answer to questions like that or, "How are you doing?" or when his mother asked, "Do you really think a checked shirt and plaid pants go together?"

"So, what did you learn from this experience?" the driver asked as he pulled away from the curb.

Fenton wanted to say he'd learned Dimmelmans had a store wide sale in February but because of the mix-up with the address Gloria Stuffelbeam had missed it. That he was relieved the Stuffelbeam problem was finally taken care of. And that he understood why Brian Alexander acted the way he did if his father treated him the way he did those on his postal route.

Instead he mumbled, "Something about mailing things I guess," and sat back in his seat. He hoped he'd remember this experience so, sometime in the future, when his son handed him a letter delivered to their house by mistake, he'd know what to do. They would hold hands as they crossed the street to the mailbox and on the way he would ask how his day at school had been.

His thoughts were interrupted when the taxi driver said, "I was kidding about the meter running, Wish Wizards Inc. will pick up the tab on this one."

Chapter 13
CURLY FLEEMAN, NEW AND USED WORDS

Fenton Alowishus Tug's mother told him, "Don't worry dear, you'll think of something," as she slid a turkey pot pie on his plate.

"It happens to me all the time," his father said from behind the evening newspaper.

"You should have decked the guy," his older brother Felix demonstrated how he would have handled the situation by smacking Fenton on the back of the head.

Fenton had told them about Friday afternoon's recess.

He'd kicked a ball over the first baseman's outstretched arms and was running hard, trying to turn a single into a double. He stepped on first base and was halfway to second when he ran into Rudy "Big Foot" Griggs.

When they collided, Fenton fell backwards but Rudy remained standing.

"Dumb move Tug," Rudy said as he caught the ball thrown by the outfielder and smacked it against Fenton's leg. "You're out and remember, nobody stretches a single into a double when Rudy's playing second base." He leaned close to Fenton's ear and whispered, "Not you. Not nobody." He stared at Fenton long enough to make sure he got the message, then jogged to the dugout.

When Fenton took his place in right field, he heard the fans of the other team yell:

*"Turn off the lights,
total up the score,
he could have made a single,
but he tried to go for more."*

He would have yelled back if he'd thought of something to say. He wondered why he could never come up with a snappy comeback the moment things happen. At home, in his room, he could think of a lot of stuff but when it was happening, his mind went blank.

Later in the afternoon, as he was getting off the school bus, the sleeve of his jacket caught in the door handle, causing him to drop his lunch box and notebook. The notebook opened when it hit the ground and he watched helplessly as the sheet of spelling words for Monday's test slid beneath a tire of the bus.

He hollered for the driver to stop but it was too late, the door had closed. The sooner Mr. Fleener got back to school the sooner his weekend started. Fenton watched his spelling work sheet, stuck to a tire, flip over and over as the bus pulled away from the curb.

A window went down and Brian Alexander yelled, "What's the matter Tug, at a loss for words?" Fenton heard Brian's buddy Andy laugh and say, "Good one."

"I wish I could think of something really clever to say," Fenton muttered as he picked up his notebook and lunch box. He shook his thermos and heard the sound of broken glass.

Fenton was confused.

He walked back to the corner of Third and Broadmore, turned around, and retraced his steps.

This was the second time he'd done it and decided he could spend the weekend walking back and forth and it wouldn't make any difference. *The Sweet Tooth*, his favorite candy store, was gone. He hadn't been down this street for a couple of weeks but buildings don't disappear do they?

Adding to his confusion was the candy store had been replaced by a paved lot with yellow stripes marking off spaces barely wide enough for a toy car. But, instead of cars, there were metal boxes painted various colors. The lids were closed and held in place by tiny padlocks.

In the center of the lot was a building the size of a telephone booth. The lower part was painted bright red, the middle was frosted glass, and the top a shade of green he'd never seen before. A pole poked through the top of the building and rose ten feet above the roof. A light that looked like an old fashioned lantern hung from a hook on top and a speaker was mounted beneath it. Above the entrance was a hand written sign that identified it as the, *"Sales Office."*

Since the candy store wasn't there, Fenton decided he'd wait and spend his allowance when he went shopping with his mother. He was startled when the speaker crackled and a man's voice boomed across the lot, "Hold your horses sir, I'm on my lunch break."

Fenton looked behind him thinking someone looking for *The Sweet Tooth* was as confused as he was but didn't see anyone.

"I'm talking to you sir," the voice from the speaker said. "Red ball cap. Khaki shorts. Striped shirt."

The question facing Fenton now was what to do. He hadn't actually seen the person whose voice he'd heard so couldn't he just wave in the direction of the sales office and holler, "That's okay, I was looking for…" That's where it got tricky, trying to find a way to say he was looking for a something that wasn't there.

No one had come out of the office so, as far as Fenton was concerned, it was a voice on a tape recorder. Someone steps on the sidewalk, breaks an invisible beam, and the tape player comes on. He figured it worked like the motion detector on the light over the backdoor of his house.

He'd convinced himself it was a recorded message so it was okay to leave when the door to the sales office opened and a short, heavyset man stepped out. He wore a blue sport coat and green pants. Part of a yellow and black checkered vest poked from beneath his coat. His shirt collar and tie were hidden by the paper napkin tucked under his chin.

"There now," the man said and became aware of the napkin when he reached out to shake Fenton's hand. He pulled it off, rolled it in a ball, and stuck it in the pocket of his coat. The pocket bulged with what Fenton figured were dozens of napkin balls.

"Sorry to keep you waiting but I was..." The man nodded as if waiting for Fenton to finish with, "eating lunch." When he didn't, the man continued. "I'm Curly Fleeman, chief cook and bottle washer at *Curly Fleeman's New and Used Words,* at your service." As he spoke he swung his arm in an arc that took in the paved lot from one side to the other. "Now, what can I do for you today?" Curly put his hand on Fenton's elbow and pulled him off the sidewalk and onto the paved surface of the lot.

"I'm not, I mean, I wasn't really..." Fenton wanted to say he didn't know how Curly could help him because he had no idea who he was or what he did.

"Can't think of what to say?" Curly nodded in a way that suggested Fenton was the last in a long line of customers who'd come to him with the same problem. He flashed a confident smile. "That's why I'm here sir. That's why, a number of years ago, while suffering from a problem similar to yours, I decided to do something about it." Fenton saw a tear form in the corner of Curly's eye, as if remembering the torment of days spent searching for the right word was painful for him to recall. He removed a napkin ball from his pocket, unfolded it, and dabbed at the corner of his eye. When he finished, he wadded it up and stuck it back in his pocket.

"But, rising from the ashes of that terrible experience, I found my calling and discovered my purpose in life." He looked at Fenton in a way that asked, you know what that purpose is don't you?

Fenton had no idea what he was talking about.

"Words sir!" Curly said as he looked proudly across the lot. **"New and used.** Boxes of them carefully selected, cataloged, and filed. Those on this side have never seen the light of day and the used ones," he turned Fenton so he was facing the other direction, "still have some of the original inflection left in them." He smiled proudly. "They're what I do sir. They're who I am and, in the end, any serious minded person will admit, they're what we are."

Curly grew silent as he continued thinking about the role words play in the affairs of man.

Fenton looked longingly at the sidewalk in front of the lot.

"Now sir, what did you have in mind when you entered my establishment this morning?" Curly pulled a napkin from his coat pocket and dabbed the perspiration that had formed on his forehead.

"I don't, I mean I wouldn't ..." Fenton stopped, tilted his head to one side and asked, "Can you do that? Buy and sell words? Don't you have them on a spelling test or use one you've heard someone say?" Since hearing Curly's voice over the speaker Fenton felt he'd been a step behind in the conversation.

"That would certainly be considered a used word, to hear it from someone. **BUT,**" he tucked the fingers of one hand in his vest pocket and raised the other in the air, **"WHY NOT BE THE FIRST TO USE IT? WHY NOT HAVE OTHERS SAY, THAT'S A GREAT WORD, I'VE GOT TO REMEMBER IT?"**

Curly's face was flushed with excitement and had a look that asked why anyone would want to play second fiddle when it came to words. He'd stomped his foot when he said, **"I'VE GOT TO REMEMBER IT."** When he finished, he loosened his tie and undid the top button of his pale green shirt.

He took Fenton's arm and led him to the new word side of the lot. He pulled a key chain from his pocket that had dozens of small keys and a tag with, *New Words* printed on it. Curly tapped his chin and hummed as he studied the boxes in front of him. He smiled, reached down and inserted a key in the padlock on a blue and white stripped box. He mumbled to himself as he flipped through the cards he'd removed from the box. "Too fancy. Not his kind of word. Not appropriate for the situation. Maybe something more..." He put the cards back in the box, snapped the lock shut, and moved further back in the lot. He stopped in front of a yellow box with an orange star on top.

He spoke excitedly as he opened the lock. "Imagine you're speaking to a group of economists and they ask your opinion on, say, the effect of a full moon on a persons chance of winning the lottery. With me so far?" Curly looked at Fenton while he picked through the cards in the box. He tapped the top of one before removing it. "You step to the microphone and say in your opinion the full moon would certainly," he held the card up for Fenton to read.

Fenton squinted. "Ag…" is as far as he got, he couldn't pronounce the rest.

Curly looked at Fenton and said, "**AGRIVATE**. You say it would certainly **AGRIVATE** the situation. It means to make things worse." He reached inside his coat pocket, pulled out a short, stubby pencil, scratched through a number on the back of the card, and wrote a new one.

"You can have this word for," he chewed on the end of the pencil before saying, "$1.25. But only **IF YOU ACT TODAY!** Otherwise it will be $1.50 like it would for everyone else. It's a perfect word, used in the newspapers a few times but I can personally guarantee they're not from around here."

"Well see, I, I mean I'm…" Fenton was lost. He couldn't pronounce the word let alone know when to use it. Even if he figured out how to pronounce it, no one in his class would know what it meant? Perky Bergbinder the 3rd would because he knows everything.

Besides, he only had fifty cents.

"Okay," Curly raised his hands in an act of surrender, "I see where you're going with this. I didn't just fall off a turnip truck." He tugged on the sleeves of his sport coat until the cuffs of his shirt weren't showing. He had the look of a man about to begin serious negotiations. "A buck five's my last offer. Take it or leave it." Fenton watched Curly mark through the last number on the card and write $1.05 beneath it.

When he saw Fenton was about to say he wasn't interested he waved his hands and told him to, "Keep your shirt on sir, I'm just getting started. To sweeten the pot and offer a deal you can't refuse, I'll throw in the word **ELOQUENT** as a gift when you buy **AGRIVATE**?"

"No, see, I'm really…" Fenton took a step back.

Curly reached in the box and pulled out another card. "To show you my heart's in the right place, I'll add **EULOGY**. Three words, one price. I guarantee you won't find a deal like that at another new and used word lot in the city."

"I'm in the third grade," Fenton blurted out. He was afraid if he didn't Curly would keep pulling out words he'd never heard before. "I don't know when I'd use words like that."

Curly looked surprised. "Don't kid a kidder sir. Your telling me someone your size is only in third…" A smile formed and a wink followed. "Kids at school make fun of you don't they?" He nodded in a way that told Fenton he knew all about it. "I was your size once." When he saw the look of surprise on Fenton's face he quickly added, "Life does that to you."

Fenton couldn't see how a man whose head barely came to his shoulders could ever have been as tall as he was. "I've only got fifty cents and was going to buy…"

Curly held up his hands telling Fenton to hold his horses. He tapped his foot and rolled his head from side to side as he considered this new piece of information. Then, all motion stopped except for his hand that slowly raised and pointed to a box on the used words side of the lot.

"My boy," he said excitedly. "your troubles are over. Your days of humiliation ended. In that box is a word I'll let you have for fifty cents and the mere possession of it will turn your life around and send you in an exciting new direction." As he talked he walked to the box he'd pointed to. He pulled out a different set of keys and found the one that fit the lock.

The box was painted an odd shade of purple and had a green footprint on top.

The lid snapped open and Curly flipped through the cards until he found the one he was looking for. He pulled it from the box, thought for a second, then removed another.

He faced Fenton and smiled the smile of a man who knew in a few minutes he'd have two shiny quarters in his pocket. He didn't say anything, he just stared at Fenton and smiled.

"What?" Fenton didn't know what else to say.

"Today my boy, because I have walked a mile in your shoes, I am going to give you not one word but two. And, I'm sure you will be delighted to learn, you can have them both for the price you'd normally pay for one."

"I don't know. See I was..." Fenton wanted to tell him about the candy store that used to be here and how, when he came by this morning he had no intention of spending his allowance on words, new or used.

But he didn't.

Curly looked over his shoulder to make sure no one was listening, afraid if they were they'd expect the same kind of deal he was giving Fenton. He lowered his voice to a whisper. "Use these words sir and no one will bother you about your shoe size, arithmetic score, or how long it takes you to run from home plate to second base." His voice grew louder. "You have my personal guarantee you'll be popular with your classmates and admired by your teachers." He stood at attention, raised his right hand like he was taking an oath and finished with, **"You might be elected captain of the chess team."**

"Well, see, I don't really play..."

"Details my boy, don't get bogged down in details. The main thing, the thing I'm trying to tell you, the thing I want you to understand is, ***these words will change your life***! You can't put a price tag on something like that?" He grabbed the front of Fenton's shirt and pulled him closer.

Fenton felt his feet slide across the pavement as he was pulled closer to the purple box. "Yes, I see, but I've only got…"

"Fifty cents? This is not about money sir, it's never been about money. Why, I'd give you these words for free if I could but I have to pay for this attractive lot and that fancy speaker up there." He pointed to the lantern mounted above the sales office. He studied the words then looked at Fenton before saying, "Fifty cents should just about cover it." He rubbed the cards on his sleeve, making sure the words were facing away from Fenton."

"I don't…" Fenton wavered.

Curly heard the hesitation in Fenton's voice and afraid he'd wriggle off the hook, plunged forward. "Listen to this and see if it doesn't knock the socks off any deal you've ever heard. I'll give your money back **IF** these words don't do everything I say they will." He paused long enough for Fenton to consider the offer before winking and adding, "How about them apples?"

"Well, I guess I…"

"Sold to the young man in the ball cap. Follow me." Curly took off at a such a fast pace Fenton had to run to keep up with him.

"What are they? How do I know they'll work?" Fenton called after Curly who'd reached the sales office and opened the door. He spun around, looked at Fenton and said, "Show me the money and I'll show you the words. It's in the fine print of the contract." Curly had changed from a guy out to make life easier for a befuddled third grader who had trouble thinking of things to say when his classmates made fun of him, to a hard-nosed salesman seconds away from closing a major deal.

Fenton thought he'd asked a reasonable question but the way Curly responded forced him to try a different approach. "How about this, show me the words and if I like them I'll give you the money."

Curly shook his head. "No can do, son. You see the words, take off, and I watch fifty cents sail off my lot. Do you think you're the first one to try that on me? Why, at the price I'm selling these words for I'm practically giving them away." Curly headed back to the purple box, pulled the key chain from his pocket, and looked at Fenton. He held the cards with the words guaranteed to change his life in one hand and the key to the box in the other. "Going once. Going tw…"

"Okay. I'll buy them." Fenton pulled two quarters from his pocket and dropped them in Curly's hand.

"Best decision you've made all morning sir," Curly spoke over his shoulder as he hurried back to the sales office. He was afraid if he waited too long Fenton would change his mind. It wouldn't be the first time someone got cold feet and backed out of a deal when they saw the words they'd purchased.

Fenton followed him and waited outside while he finished the paperwork. He heard a cash register ring, paper being torn from a pad, and a box sliding across the floor. It was quiet for a moment, then the door opened and Curly stepped out holding a lime green envelope.

"You said you're in third grade. Right?" He looked at Fenton and raised his eyebrows.

Fenton nodded yes.

"All right, let's see, something simple." He tapped his foot and put a finger on his chin as he thought of an example Fenton would understand. "On the way to the pencil sharpener you bump a desk sending a girl's books sailing across the floor. Some wise guy in the room…"

"Brian," Fenton added trying to make the example as real as possible.

"Okay, Brian walks up and…"

"Alexander. His name is Brian Alexander." Fenton had no trouble picturing the incident Curly was describing because it happened Friday afternoon.

"I'll stick with Brian if it's all right with you We don't want this to get too complicated." Curly paused, looked at the ground and mumbled, "Let's see, where was I?"

"I bumped a desk." Fenton blushed after saying it.

"Exactly," Curly looked at him and smiled. "So Brian stands up and says you couldn't walk through an empty room with the lights on without tripping over something." Curly walked back and forth and smacked his hands together as he reached the end of the story. He bumped the side of the sales office with his hip to help Fenton visualize the scene he was describing.

"That's what he said." Fenton was astonished. Curly described the scene exactly as it happened.

"And you said?" Curly rolled his pudgy hand suggesting Fenton finish for him.

Fenton blushed and ducked his head. "Nothing."

"Because?" Curly leaned toward Fenton.

"Everyone was looking and my mind went blank. I felt stupid." Fenton looked down and studied the yellow stripes on the pavement.

They were silent for a moment, then Curly opened the envelope and pulled out two cards. "Next time, whatever the situation, use these." He handed Fenton the cards.

Fenton looked at them and then back at Curly. "Case dismissed?"

"No my boy, not case dismissed. Let me help you. The words are **CEASE**," he replaced the first card with the second, "*and* **DESIST**." They both mean to stop but when used together, they pack a bigger punch." Curly put the cards and sales receipt back in the envelope and handed it to Fenton.

Fenton stared at the envelope for a moment before saying, "I don't know. Maybe I should…"

"All sales are final. You can't get your money back until you've tried them." He put the envelope in Fenton's hand and folded his fingers around it. "They're keepers my boy, trust me. Use these words and Brian Alexander won't know what hit him. To add icing to the cake and show you my heart's in the right place, I'll throw in the word *and* for free. You can't beat that kind of deal with a stick."

He looked Fenton in the eye, said, "Enjoy," then stepped in the sales office and closed the door.

Fenton stood for a moment, not sure what to do. He looked at the envelope and got the sinking feeling he'd thrown his allowance down the drain.

The speaker overhead crackled and Curly announced, "We'll be closing in approximately a minute and twenty seconds folks. Please clear the lot."

Fenton looked around and mumbled, "Folks?" when he discovered he was the only one there.

Fenton kept telling himself how stupid he'd been as he walked the four blocks to his house. He couldn't believe he'd spent his candy money on two words he could have looked up in the dictionary. Well, maybe not those words because he'd never heard them before but it was the idea that bugged him. And the part about, he changed his voice to sound like Curly's, "I'll throw in **and** for free," only made him feel worse, he'd used the word *and* a bunch of times.

He stopped walking when the thought hit him that he was as dumb as Brian Alexander said he was.

When he got home he went straight to his room and put the envelope in his desk drawer. He thought about tearing it up and throwing it in the trash but knew if he did, he wouldn't be able to get his money back when he returned it to *Curly Fleeman's New and Used Words* lot Monday after school.

The rest of the weekend was uneventful and before he knew it, his mother knocked on the door to his room and said breakfast would be ready in five minutes. For Fenton it announced the start of another week of shame and humiliation. Being upset about wasting his money on two useless words was replaced by worry about what Brian Alexander was going to make fun of.

It didn't take long.

While Ms Chalmer was taking attendance and counting the number of kids buying lunch, Fenton asked his friend Myron Cleeg how long *The Sweet Tooth* had been gone.

Myron shrugged he didn't know because he lived on the other side of school.

His question didn't go unnoticed. Brian Alexander heard enough to know Fenton was about to make a repeat appearance on the *Dumb and Dumber Show*.

"What's that about *The Sweet Tooth*?" Brian asked loud enough to be heard by everyone in the room.

He leaned forward, inches away from Fenton's ear. "Duh. Could it be you were on the wrong street Fen-tone?" Brian had a dopey look on his face and was pointing at Fenton. "Hey Andy," he called to his friend, "you know what this is?" He made two fingers into legs and walked them up one side of Fenton's head and down the other.

Andy looked confused and shook his head, letting Brian know he didn't.

"A trip over the weak end." He turned to the guy next to him, pointed to Fenton's head and repeated, "The weak end. Get it?" The kid he was talking to laughed, put his hand up, and they high fived each other. Several seated near them laughed and repeated the joke for those who'd missed it the first time.

Fenton's mind was going a mile a minute. Words zipped in and out of his thoughts so fast he couldn't keep track of them. He pictured Curly Fleeman reaching into the metal box and pulling out two cards.

Brian leaned forward. "What's a matter Fentino, cat got your tongue?"

Fenton watched Curly pull the cards from the lime green envelope and slowly turn them so he could see the words printed on them.

"Whoops, my mistake," Brian said as he leaned close to Fenton's ear. He jumped back with a look of horror on his face and his hands pressed against his head. "Egad, the cat didn't stop with his tongue, it ate his brain too."

Everyone around them laughed.

Fenton stood, but instead of being embarrassed and running out of the room, he turned and faced Brian. "**CEASE *and***

DESIST," he said with all the authority he could muster. Brian plopped back in his chair with his mouth open. This was the first time in three years Fenton hadn't hung his head, blushed, and kept quiet as he fired away with sarcastic comments.

"Your conduct has **AGRIVATED** the tension between us." Fenton didn't know what was happening. He wasn't even thinking as words flew out of his mouth and there was nothing he could do to stop them.

"You think your **ELOQUENT** but if you insist on making fun of me I'll be asked to deliver your **EULOGY**."

Those seated around them were silent. The look on Brian's face had changed from amusement, to astonishment, and finally, fear.

A girl in a seat next to Brian turned to her friend and whispered, "I hadn't noticed before but Fenton's kind of cute."

Her friend said, "I love the way he uses words."

They giggled and said, "He is so cool," at the same time.

Several seated near him said, "Way to go Fenton. Brian's been asking for that for a long time."

Ms Chalmer stepped over and asked if there was a problem. Fenton looked at Brian then back at her. "Not any more."

She stepped around Fenton and looked at Brian. "How about you, everything okay?"

Brian nodded and for the first time in his life, couldn't think of anything to say.

The rest of the day was more than Fenton could have hoped for. At lunch he was walking to his usual table at the far end of the cafeteria when some of the boys in his room asked him to join them. All they could talk about was the look on Brian's face when Fenton told him to **CEASE *and* DESIST**. They asked where he came up with that but instead of answering,

Fenton shrugged and stuck a spoon in his chocolate pudding. At recess he was picked first to be on a kickball team and during the last hour of class a girl walked by and dropped a slip of paper with her name and phone number on his desk. She'd written, "Call me!" on the front of the note and underlined it twice.

When the school bus reached his stop, Fenton was the first one off. He sprinted the block and a half to his house and ran up the steps to his room. He reached in the back of his closet and pulled out the jar where he kept the money he was saving for a new bicycle. He pulled out two dollars, spun the lid shut. and stuck the jar back where it had been.

He ran down the stairs and hollered to whoever might be listening, "I'll be back in a few minutes." As he hurried down the street he thought if fifty cents could make such a change in what the kids at school thought of him, what would two dollars do? He couldn't believe the power those words had. Curly promised they would change his life and they had.

He rounded the corner and started toward the end of the block for *Curly Fleeman's New and Used Words* but slowed as he tried to make sense of the scene in front of him. Where the lot had been was the familiar brick front of *The Sweet Tooth*. And, in place of the pole with the light and loud speaker, he saw the familiar red and white candy cane with neon lights that blinked their way from bottom to top.

He pushed the door to the shop open and almost immediately Trudy, the wife of the owner said, "Long time no see Fenton. What have you been up to?"

Usually Fenton said, "Hi Trudy what's today's special?" Instead he stood, trying to figure out what was going on. He knew he wasn't the quickest thinker in the world but once he started to work on a problem he saw it through to a conclusion.

"Ah, Trudy, has anything, I don't know, changed around here recently?" Fenton pressed his face against the plate glass window trying to see in back of the store. Maybe Curly's lot was behind the building.

"Well sure Fenton, a lot has changed since you were here last. The chocolate covered cherries weren't selling so we replaced them with pecan nuggets. And the sugared..." Trudy was pointing to a lower shelf in the display case when Fenton interrupted. "I mean really changed, like..." he hesitated, afraid to say like your building being replaced by a parking lot with boxes that contained new and used words.

"Those are pretty big changes for us Fenton. You don't just pull chocolate covered cherries off the shelf on a whim. You have to think about..." When she saw the look on Fenton's face she asked, "Are you okay?"

"Yea, I guess, I just thought..." Nothing made sense to him. Things were happening too fast. He'd had such a great day and thought if he could buy a few more words, maybe venture into the new word section, he could keep the momentum going for another day or two. The thought passed through his mind that he might not have to spend the entire two dollars; Curly might have a deal or two up his sleeve.

While he was standing in the middle of the room, staring at the tiles in the floor Norris, Trudy's husband, walked from the back carrying a tray of maple nut fudge. "Hey Fenton, I didn't know you were here. Want to sample the fudge?" Norris set the tray down and began sliding the slabs of fudge into the refrigerated showcase.

"No thanks Norris, I don't...."

"Something bothering you Fenton?" Norris couldn't remember Fenton ever turning down a free sample of his favorite kind of fudge.

"Yea, I guess, I'll just..." Fenton shrugged, turned toward the door and said, "See you around."

He pulled on the handle and the door was halfway open when Norris called out, "Hey Fenton, I almost forgot. Some guy dropped this off for you." He pulled a lime green envelope from under the cash register and handed it to him. "Funny looking fella. He said he'd been in the candy business himself and owned a store like ours. Never met him before but I thought he was going to talk my leg off. He ended up buying fifty cents worth of chocolate covered raisins and paid with two quarters like you do."

Fenton took the envelope and saw his name written in big letters across the front.

"Gee, thanks Norris, this is great, just great," he said as he hurried out of the store and headed for home.

He sat at his desk with the envelope propped against his stack of school books. He traced a finger along the word *Fenton* printed on the front and then decided he'd waited long enough. He was about to slip his finger under the wax seal on the back when he saw a circle formed by the words Wish Wizards Inc. and in the center, the wishbone of a turkey.

"He was a wish wizard?" Fenton said out loud as he opened the envelope and removed the card with a word printed in bold, black letters. "**WORDSMITH**," Fenton read out loud. Below the word he could make out Curly's shaky signature, written with the blunt end of a stubby pencil.

"Wordsmith?" Fenton thought for a moment, reached for his dictionary and flipped to the W's. His finger skimmed past wart and widget until he came to wordsmith. "A person who works with words," he read out loud.

He turned the card over and looked at the back. He saw a series of numbers, each having a line drawn through it. The top number was two dollars, below that a dollar fifty and, at the bottom of the list he saw, "No charge."

"How about that," he said as he sat back in his chair, "I'm a wordsmith."

His mother hollered from the bottom of the stairs. "Did you say something dear?"

"Not really," he called back then quickly added, "but I might. You never know."

Chapter 14
THE VISIT

 Fenton Alowishus Tug crouched behind a papier-mâché cactus. He was wearing fake deerskin trousers and cardboard moccasins. A red feather was stuck in a beaded headband and his face was covered with war paint. As soon as the scouting party left the stage it would be his turn to sing. While he waited he wished for the hundredth time he'd been home with the flu or a sprained ankle the day Daniel Farb came to Cody Elementary. The first notes of music reached backstage and he knew he couldn't put it off any longer; it was show time.

 It started the morning Ms Chalmer announced a special guest was going to visit her class and she wanted them to be on their best behavior. The first sign bad things were about to happen was when Fenton's normally cool and collected teacher stumbled over words and tugged nervously on a sleeve of her blouse.

 She'd finished saying "best behavior" when the door opened and a short, heavyset man wearing a beret and cape with a red lining strolled in. He approached Ms Chalmer, took her hand, kissed it and said, "Enchanted." She blushed and several girls in the front row giggled.

 He continued holding her hand as he turned to the class and said, "Good morning." Said is the wrong word to describe what he did, sang is more like it. And the worst part was, after singing it, he placed a hand behind his ear, expecting the class to answer.

 "Good," a few managed to say. "Morning," came from others.

Their response was greeted with a shaking head and disappointed look. "Let's try that again shall we?" he said as he thrust his hand toward them and sang, "Good morning," expecting the class to return his greeting. The girls were the first to catch on and sang, "Good morning."

The visitor let go of Ms Chalmer's hand and asked the class, "Did you hear it? Were you listening?" Before they could answer, he pulled a pitch pipe from the pocket of his cape and blew on it. He made a high note followed by a low one then looked at the class. No one knew what to do. Were they supposed to hum the notes he'd played? Sing them? Say "Good" using the high note and "Morning" the low? Or the other way around?

"Together," he announced and repeated, "Good morning," using the same notes he'd played. He smiled and wiggled his fingers, encouraging them to sing with him. It took several tries but they managed to do it.

"This time the girls sing good and the boys morning." He pointed to the girls who eagerly sang their part but it didn't work as well with the boys. Some were off key. Some weren't about to sing with the girls watching. Only three, Brian Alexander, Billy Gilsky, and Fenton did.

The visitor hurried to where the boys were sitting, crouched in front of their desks and pointed to the girls who sang, "Good." He closed his eyes and listened as the boys sang, "Morning."

He clapped his hands, jumped to his feet, and started to the door. "Follow me," he said over his shoulder. The three boys stood. "Not all of you," the visitor said as he spun around and pointed at Fenton, "just you."

Ms Chalmer nodded it was okay for Fenton to go and he had to run to catch up with the visitor who was already halfway down the hallway.

When they entered the auditorium Fenton saw other students, several from each class, huddled in small groups. Rather than take the steps, the visitor jumped from the floor to the stage. The students gasped and looked at Principal Logan to see what he would do. There were rules to follow when you came to the auditorium. Walk down the aisle don't run. Stand quietly until your teacher tells you to sit down. Don't put gum on the bottom of your seat. And, last but not least, never, ever jump from the floor to the stage. They expected Mr. Logan to make him go back and use the stairs on either side of the stage.

Instead, he shook the visitors hand, gestured for him to sit on the bench beside the piano, and urged the students to move to the first two rows. "I'm sure you're wondering why you've been invited here this morning." He raised his eyebrows, an expression that was greeted by nods. "Of all the students in our school you have been selected to be part of *The Visit*, an original theatrical production with words and music by Stemsville's own, Daniel Farb." When he finished he stepped aside and gestured to the one who, until that moment, had been a stranger to those in the auditorium.

Some clapped. Others didn't know what they were supposed to do.

Daniel Farb stood and walked confidently to the front of the stage. He waited for complete silence before starting. When they were seated he said, "An historic event took place in Stemsville one hundred years ago. Buffalo Bill Cody brought his Wild West Show to town. Featured in the production were Annie Oakley, Sitting Bull, and a cast of hundreds." He paused, walked back to the piano, and sat down. "What you may not know is my grandfather, Winston Elijah Farb, attended the show. From that experience, brief as it was, he became a collector of authentic Indian paraphernalia. Perhaps your class has visited the *Winston Farb Gallery of Indian Artifacts*?" He expected nods of recognition from the students but received shaking heads and confused looks. They'd visited a farm and an art gallery but not the place he mentioned. The boys were sure they'd remember going to a museum with bows and arrows on display.

"To honor my grandfather and commemorate the event, I have written *The Visit*." He put his hands on the piano keys and played as he sang,

"You came in peace, to this pleasant land.
We greeted you with an open hand."

His left hand played a thump, thump to imitate the sound of drums while his right traced the melody.

The rest of the morning was spent assigning parts. Because the kids in the sixth grade were bigger, they were selected to play Buffalo Bill, Annie Oakley, and Sitting Bull. Nonspeaking roles were divided among the other students. Fenton began to relax; all the parts had been handed out and the important thing was he hadn't been given one.

The students grew quiet while Daniel Farb tapped a finger against his chin and mumbled, "I wonder if…" He walked toward those not selected for the play, studied them for a moment, pointed at Fenton and said, "You, will be Sitting Bull as a boy."

As Fenton joined others onstage, he heard Daniel Farb say to those he'd been sitting with, "Don't feel bad you weren't selected, there are only so many parts." He thanked them for waiting patiently and finished with, "You may return to your classrooms." Fenton watched them go and was saddened by the thought that if it weren't for a last minute decision to include a scene Daniel Farb had removed earlier that morning, he would be going with them.

It was the final practice and only cast members were allowed to attend. Fenton was uncomfortable. The fake deerskin pants he'd been given to wear were meant for someone bigger than him. His mother had pulled them together at the waist and held them in place with a safety pin. His father used duct tape to patch a worn place in the sole of his cardboard moccasins. And, though he liked to sing along with the radio in his room with the door closed, the thought of doing it in front of an auditorium of grown ups and students made his stomach churn.

He had one song, "What will become of me?" at the start of the show. And, if the pressure to appear in front of an audience wasn't enough, he'd been reminded several times by the director, "You're performance sets the tone for the rest of the show."

Why he had to hide behind a fake cactus plant while the cavalry rode by he didn't know but he was there now, waiting for his cue. A sergeant would report to his commander, "Ain't no injuns in these parts sir." After the soldiers left, Fenton was to run on stage, look around to make sure they were gone, and sing.

"I wish I could get out of this," Fenton whispered and almost immediately felt something slip into his hand. He looked down and saw a bar of soap shaped like a gun.

"Flash it around, no one'll know the difference," someone behind him said in a gruff voice. Fenton turned and saw a tall, skinny man with an enormous mustache, wearing a cowboy hat.

"What?" Fenton whispered. The stranger sighed and raised his bushy eye brows. To him it was about the element of surprise and Fenton was about to lose it. "You've got to get a move on kid. If you let the soldier finish his report, the horse has left the barn."

"Who are you?" Fenton whispered.

"U.S. Marshall Willard Tweet, retired. You wished. I'm here. So head um up and move um out."

"Where? Do what?" With the action on stage and the odd way Marshall Tweet pronounced words, Fenton was having trouble figuring out what he was supposed to do.

"Jump the fence and ride into the sunset. I carved the gun myself." Marshal Tweet gave him a shove and said, "Skedaddle, you're burning daylight."

Fenton stumbled to the center of the stage and held the soap gun up for everyone to see.

Marshal Tweet said so only Fenton could hear, "I'm busting out of here and the first one to move gets it." When he finished Fenton repeated what he said.

One of the soldiers laughed and pointed at Fenton. "Who you trying to fool Tug? No one's going to get it from a gun made out of a bar of soap"

Daniel Farb, unaware of what was going on said, "Wait for the sergeant to give his report Mr. Tug, we've been over this several times." To the others on stage he said, "Take it back to line four, 'ain't no injuns in these parts sir.' And Fenton, throw that thing away, Sitting Bull used a bow and arrow, not a gun."

When Fenton returned to the cactus plant, Marshal Willard Tweet said, "Boy howdy, the guy's quicker than blue blazes. I didn't think he'd figure it out that fast."

The first sign of trouble came when Mr. Blaine, the custodian, arrived for work and found an arrow stuck in the front door of the school. Attached to the arrow was a note that demanded all the items in the *Winston Farb Gallery* be returned to the original owners. It also said the tribal council would not leave the reservation until they received word their demand had been met.

Mr. Blaine looked out the window by the front door and saw a teepee on the front lawn. Men wearing Indian costumes, milled around, drinking coffee from Styrofoam cups, and talking on mobile phones. He followed the procedure set by the school board and reported the problem to Principal Logan.

Later that morning when he took the trash to the dumpster, he saw a team of cavalry reenactors assembled on the playground setting up tents and practicing close order drill.

It wasn't long before a van from *KBOP,* the local radio station, rolled to a stop and *The Voice Of Stemsville*, Winwood Beach stepped out, microphone in hand. "The skies over Stemsville are troubled this morning. A showdown has developed at Buffalo Bill Cody Elementary between groups of angry protesters. It's the typical standoff scenario with neither side willing to back down."

He hurried across the playground and stopped when he came to a reenactor wearing the an officer's uniform. "First Lieutenant Burley Grim," the officer answered proudly when Winwood asked his name. Without prompting he added, "We're protesting the lack of authentic clothing and equipment in tonight's production of *The Visit*. The portrayal of the cavalry as insensitive to the condition of the American Indian is an insult to the brave soldiers of our historic past.

"Why, I understand some kid," he stopped and hollered to another reenactor, "what's the kids name?" The one he was talking to shrugged and mumbled he didn't know. "Anyway, I understand the soldiers looking for Sitting Bull don't see him and he's like ten feet away, hiding behind a specie of cactus not indigenous to our neck of the woods."

"So basically you're saying…" Winwood tilted the microphone toward Burley who finished with, "Do it right or don't do it at all." He started to walk away but remembered something and came back. "Word has it they're using weapons made out of soap."

The final blow came when Daniel Farb received a registered letter from the law firm of Leaner and Meaner. After making his way through 14 pages of complicated legal jargon, he discovered he was being sued by someone named Cyril Gimble for stealing the words and music for the opening song, What will become of me? "A song the author said he composed ten years ago as part of his *Salute To Our Founders* series."

Fenton was relieved when a parent of one of the kids in the play called and said the performance was off due to a disturbance and unless things were straightened out, no one was allowed near the school.

Mayor Middleton honked his horn to get the attention of the police officer blocking the entrance to the school parking lot. The officer recognized the mayor's personal license plate, **IWRK4U**, and waved him through.

As soon as the car skidded to a stop, he hopped out and Principal Logan walked over to meet him. Instead of the usual warm handshake and, "How 's it going Andy?" the Mayor barked, "What's the problem?"

Principal Logan explained it was about the school play and he had the leaders of the protesting groups in his office. The mayor pushed passed him and walked briskly to the school building. When he entered the principal's office, he saw the feuding parties seated with their backs to each other.

Representing the reenactors was Burley Grim of *Grim and Barret Wealth Management.* Across from him wearing leggings, moccasins, and a cowhide shirt was Marty Climber partner in *Walker and Climber Janitorial Service.*

"Marty!" Mayor Middleton said as he grabbed his hand and shook it. He crossed the room and did the same with Burley. He moved to Principal Logan's chair, sat down, and put his elbows on the desk. "I'm speaking at *The Daughters of Stemsville* brunch in fifteen minutes so what do we have to do to put a lid on this can of worms?"

He looked from one to the other and when neither answered said, "Burley?"

"The uniforms worn by the soldiers are not authentic. The weapons they carry are made of soap and no effort was made to match them with the period. They know nothing of field tactics employed by the U.S. Cavalry or have the slightest notion of close order drill." He could have gone on but stopped when the mayor held up his hand and asked, "Were you around when the school put on *The Wizard of Oz*? Auntie Em sought shelter from a paper tornado. And due to a case of stage fright, the role of Dorothy was played by a boy." He leaned forward and opened his hands. "It's a grade school play Burley, not a Hollywood production."

Burley shrugged, reluctant to give in but willing to admit the mayor had a point.

He turned to Marty and asked, "What's your beef?"

"They use the word injun to describe a noble race who…" Is as far as he got because Mayor Middleton was out of his chair, standing in the doorway, and hollering for his aide to bring a script to the principal's office, "Now!" When he returned he dropped the script on Principal Logan's desk, read through it, and every place the word injun showed up, he crossed it out and wrote Indian.

"There's one other thing," Marty said and added a note of his own.

When he handed it the script back, the mayor put his initials next to each change, stood and asked, "We done here?"

When the two combatants nodded yes, he left the room and instructed his aide to "Get Farb on the phone."

Fenton was in his room rearranging his marble collection when a secretary from the mayor's office delivered an envelope to his house. The play was back on and Daniel Farb had rewritten his solo. It was now called "What will I become?" A sticky note on the first page of music said it was to be, "Sung to the tune of Yankee Doodle Dandy."

"Remember, out of all the students they picked you," his mother told him as she dropped him off at school.

"There's no business like show business," his father said as he handed him his outfit for the play.

His brother Felix was going to tell him to, "Break a leg," but decided not to. He was afraid Fenton would take him seriously and see it as a way out of an uncomfortable situation.

Fenton watched them drive away and wished he was going with them.

Those attending the play were surprised when they were directed to their parking place by local men in Indian outfits. As they moved to the school they saw a teepee on the front lawn where refreshments would be served during the intermission. Their amazement continued when they entered the building and saw the front hallway lined with cavalry reenactors. 1st Lieutenant Burley Grim snapped to attention as they approached the auditorium door, removed his sword from its scabbard, and following the illustrations in *The Sword And It's Uses* from the *1880 Cavalry Officers Handbook*, saluted them.

Fenton took his place behind the cactus as members of the cavalry straightened their uniforms and practiced their lines. He felt someone crawl alongside him and recognized the voice of Marshal Tweet when he said, "Howdy pardner."

"How are you going to get me out of this?" Fenton asked then jumped when the school orchestra played the opening number and watched the curtains slowly rise revealing an auditorium filled with students and their parents. All the seats were taken and those with cameras stood in back ready to record the event.

Marshal Tweet whispered, "When you're caught between a rock and a hard place I've discovered sometimes you can talk your way out of it but other times you just have to bite the bullet and do what needs to be done." He paused, shook his head, and finished with, "I'm afraid this is one of those times."

Fenton looked over his shoulder and was going to ask if that was the best he could do, but discovered U.S. Marshall Willard Tweet was gone.

He was on his own.

The student in the sergeant's uniform stepped forward and read from the revised script. "There ain't no sign of that noble race of people who inhabited this land before we drove them out sir." He finished his report with a salute, then the left the stage with the rest of the search party.

Fenton heard the first notes of *Yankee Doodle Dandy* and with no back up plan or help from Wish Wizards, Inc., he stepped from behind the cactus and started to sing.

Chapter 15
PLAYGROUND WIZARD

Fenton Alowishus Tug couldn't sleep.

He'd been tossing and turning for hours and even after putting on his headphones and listening to his favorite song on his iPod, he couldn't drown out the voice of his friend Billy Gilsky.

It was the usual afternoon kickball game at school and Fenton was up. There were two outs with a runner at third. All he had to do was kick a ground ball between the first and second basemen, the runner would score, he would be lifted to the shoulders of his teammates, and carried off the field.

Several things happened that prevented his dream from becoming a reality.

As he stepped to the plate the third baseman hollered, "Blue 22," and the outfielders ran to the edge of the infield. The pitcher rolled the ball smooth and slow, not fast and bouncy like he wanted. And, last but not least, the fans of the other team yelled,

"Fenton Tug
is at the plate,
he tried to go to right field
but couldn't kick it straight."

With the movement of the fielders and jeers from the crowd, Fenton took his eyes off the ball and caught it with the sole of his shoe, not the toe. The ball bounced to the first baseman who stepped on the base and hollered, "You're out!"

That wasn't what was keeping him awake; it wasn't the first time he'd let the team down in a pressure situation. What was, was the voice of Billy Gilsky telling everyone he met, "He kicked it right to the guy. There were holes in the outfield you could drive a school bus through. There were gaps in the infield the size of a two car garage and he kicked it right to the guy."

In the past Fenton had been falsely accused of looking at someone's paper during a test and throwing Lenny Gilstrap's eraser out the window but this time Billy was right. He'd assumed the infield would go into the Tug Shift before the pitcher rolled the ball. He expected the first and second basemen to move to their right like they usually do when he's up…but they didn't, they stayed where they were. And, he thought Myron Kleeg would roll the ball the way he asked for it but he hadn't.

The last thing he whispered before finally dropping off to sleep was, "I wish I hadn't kicked it right to the guy."

When he got home from school the next day his mother told him something had come for him in the mail and she put it in his room. He ran up the stairs, opened the door, and saw a package the size of a shoe box on his desk. It was covered with stickers that warned postal workers the content was **Fragile! Do not drop!** His name was printed on the front and someone had stuck a sticker with "*Another Quality Product From Colossal Computing,*" in the return address spot. He held the package to his ear and was going to shake it but stopped when he saw someone had written "**Do Not Shake**" on the side with a felt tipped pen.

He tore off the wrapping paper, removed a brightly colored box, and saw **Batteries Included** printed on the top. He lifted the lid and found a device the size of a credit card. The front looked like the screen on his electronic game player. When he turned it over, he saw a piece of paper with an arrow pointing to a note that said, **"Press here."** He did and the screen came to life. Tiny dots swirled around like windblown snow that eventually came together to form the words, *"Playground Wizard, 1st Edition."*

The screen stayed that way for a moment, turned to snow again, then *"Amaze your teammates and baffle your opponents"* appeared. The words dissolved and he saw three fuzzy figures sitting at what looked like a table. One of them moved off the screen and almost immediately, he heard his mother holler, "Supper's ready," from the foot of the stairs.

The figure returned to the screen and it took a moment for him to make the connection. He was looking at the dinner table downstairs and the figures he saw were his mother, father, and brother.

He decided to run an experiment to make sure he was right. He opened the door to his room and hollered, "What'd you say?" He glanced at the screen and saw the figure that had just returned, leave and reappear at the foot of the stairs. "I said supper's ready and the salmon croquets are getting cold."

He told her he'd be right down.

He hurried down the stairs and was about to go to the dining room when the doorbell rang. "I'll get it," he hollered and opened the door. Standing on the porch was an overweight mailman wearing a hat too small for his head. His face was flushed from climbing the front steps.

"Fenton Rug?" the mailman gasped as he fanned his face with his hat.

Fenton nodded. The mailman set the bag he was carrying on the porch, leaned against the porch rail, and waited for his breathing to return to normal. "They wrote the wrong address on the form and I've been all over the neighborhood. The main thing is I'm here now so everything's okay."

"Can I help you," Fenton glanced at his name tag and finished with, "Lester?"

"Who?" the mailman looked over his shoulder thinking someone had followed him up the steps. It took him a moment to realize Fenton was talking to him. When he did, he leaned forward and whispered, "The question is, can I help you?"

Fenton stepped back as Lester moved closer. "Am I interrupting something? Were you about to leave? Cleaning your room? Watching television?"

"I was on my way to supper." Fenton pointed in the direction of the dining room.

"I can wait," Lester said as he opened the screen door and stepped inside, "in your room. Take your time. Enjoy your meal. It will give me time to set things up."

"Set things..." before Fenton could stop him, Lester climbed the stairs, dragging the mailbag behind him.

"We're waiting," his father hollered. Fenton watched the door to his room close then joined his family at the table. As he sat down his father asked who was at the door. Fenton shrugged and mumbled he had the wrong address. He wasn't about to tell him it was a postman named Lester who, at the moment, was in his room setting something up.

After supper, he complimented his mother on the wonderful meal and asked to be excused. When he got to his room, he cautiously opened the door and saw Lester sitting at his desk, studying the list of spelling words for tomorrow's test. When

Fenton entered, he stood and removed his hat. "Okay, the first thing you need to know is I'm not a mailman. I work for *Colossal Computing* in the TI department." He removed the U. S. Postal Service patch from his jacket, revealing an oval with the *Colossal Computing* logo; two lower case c's.

"You got that wrong Lester, it's the IT department. Information technology." Fenton said it like he'd exposed another lie he'd told.

Lester shook his head. "It stands for technical information. And, my name isn't Lester, it's Chip."

"Your name is Chip and you work with computers?" Fenton said sarcastically as he moved to the door he planned to open and usher Lester or Chip or whoever he was out.

Chip ignored the comment and got to the reason for his visit. "You received a package today." He held up the box the *Playground Wizard, 1ˢᵗ Edition* came in.

Fenton nodded, not sure where he was going with the question.

"The contents? The thing that came in the box is where?"

Fenton removed the device from his pocket and held it up for Chip to see.

"We need it back," Chip said and held out his hand.

"Why? What's wrong with it?"

Chip sighed and sat down in Fenton's chair. "It was sent by mistake. There's a, ah, problem. A snag. A glitch in the wiring." He reached in the bag next to his chair, pulled out a box that looked like the one Fenton opened earlier and slid it across the desk.

"They're the same. The boxes." Fenton said, confused.

"They look the same, but they're not." Chip opened the box and removed a pair of glasses like the ones Fenton was wearing. "Trade you," he said and handed them to Fenton.

Fenton wasn't about to fall for it. He'd traded lots of things with kids at school. Kickball hero cards. Sandwiches at lunch. Marbles and sling shots at recess. But, and this is an important point, when he traded he got something he didn't have. He had a pair of glasses, he didn't have a *Playground Wizard, 1st Edition* that showed what was happening in the dining room downstairs.

Chip frowned, put the glasses back in the box, and leaned forward. "I didn't want to tell you this but you've forced my hand, backed me into a corner, and sealed off the exits." He clasped his hands and thought for a moment searching for the best way to start. "Once upon a time there was a boy who loved to play kickball."

The moment he mentioned kickball he had Fenton's attention.

"He played with his friends at recess and when school was out he joined a summer league."

Fenton blinked. He played kickball at recess and was on a team during the summer.

"One afternoon," Chip continued, "in a particularly hard fought game, *the person in the story* came to home plate with two outs and a runner at third."

Fenton shook his head and thought, this can't be happening. Chip was describing yesterday's game like he'd been there. But there were just kids in the stands. If Chip had been there he was sure he would have seen him. A guy his size couldn't sit with a bunch of third graders and go unnoticed.

"To make a long story short, cut to the chase, and keep from drawing this sad story out longer than absolutely necessary, the kicker, *someone you've never met*, kicked a fly ball to center field…"

"That's not what happened," Fenton blurted out. He was on his feet and moving toward Chip. "It was a grounder to the first baseman."

Chip waved his hands, urging Fenton to take it easy. "Did I say this was about you? Didn't I mention it happened to someone a long time ago?"

"Yes but sometimes, when my parents want to teach me something, they tell stories like that." Fenton was surprised when Chip wiggled his fingers, urging Fenton to come closer. He looked over his shoulder like he was afraid someone was listening and whispered, "This isn't about you, it's about a boy named Eldon."

"Eldon?" Fenton asked and Chip nodded. Fenton went through the names of the kids in Ms Chalmer's class before saying, "I don't know anyone named Eldon."

"That's because you think this is about you." Chip tapped his chin, mumbled, "Where was I," then snapped his fingers when he remembered. "Eldon was embarrassed and confused. He'd been so afraid of making the last out he failed to notice the first baseman hadn't shifted toward second."

He was there, Fenton was sure of it. This wasn't about a kid named Eldon, it was about him. How else could he know about the Tug Shift?

"You're missing the point," Chip said calmly.

"Which is?" Fenton asked.

"These," Chip said as he removed the glasses from the box, "and the rest of the story."

Fenton sat down on the edge of his bed and mumbled, "Okay."

"And by okay you mean?" Chip raised his eyebrows.

"Finish the story," Fenton said and added, "please."

"So this boy.."

"Eldon."

Chip nodded. "Felt so bad about what he'd done, he never played kickball again." Chip stopped and waited so long Fenton was about to say, "Is that it?" before starting again. "Time past and Eldon, grown now, started a company called *Colossal Computing*." When he mentioned the name of the company he stood, faced the bedroom window, and saluted. He returned to the desk and sat down. "He never forgot the experience and when he heard what happened to…"

"Eldon was there? At the game?"

"Heard," Chip corrected him. "When he *heard* what happened to you he went to his laboratory, worked through the night, produced that," he pointed to the *Playground Wizard, 1st Edition* Fenton was holding, "and these," he held up the glasses.

"Why?" Fenton couldn't figure out why a complete stranger would create not one but two devices because some kid he'd never met had a bad day playing kickball.

"At last," Chip sighed, "we've come to the reason I'm here." He took off Fenton's glasses, put on the one's he'd taken from the box and asked, "What do you think?"

Fenton looked around. As far as he could tell, nothing had changed. The spelling words on his desk looked the same as they did with his old glasses. The poster on the wall of Quantos, the greatest kickball player in the world, was the same. "There's no difference," he said and felt the first twinge of anger when he realized he'd traded a perfectly good device for something that didn't work.

"Seriously?" Chip asked as he reached over and touched the lens in front of Fenton's right eye. Suddenly Fenton found he was looking at the same dining room table he'd seen on the other device.

"I don't get it," Fenton moaned like he'd missed something important Chip said.

"You don't get it because I haven't explained the features of the *Playground Wizard, 2nd Edition*."

"2nd Edition?" Fenton repeated feebly.

"1st Edition," Chip said lifting the hand held device. "2nd Edition," he added as he reached over and touched the left lens of Fenton's glasses. "Eldon thought it would be too clumsy, clunky is the technical term, to carry a computing device in your hand while playing in a high pressure kickball game so he put the same incredible technology in your glasses." The instant Chip touched the lens things returned to normal.

"Okay." Fenton gave his usual response when he didn't know what to say.

"Okay?" Chip repeated incredulously. "You're holding a device electronic enthusiasts would stand in line for hours to get their hands on and okay all you can say?"

Fenton shrugged, he hadn't thought past okay. "How's it work?"

Chip reached in his mailbag and removed what looked to Fenton like the flash cards he makes when practicing for a geography test. He cleared his throat and said, "Introducing the *Playground Wizard 2nd Edition*, a product of *Colossal Computing*." It sounded like he was making a sales presentation at an electronics convention. He turned the first card over and read the second. "Amaze your teammates and baffle your opponents by kicking it where they ain't."

He put the cards down and asked, "You're familiar with the quotation aren't you? When Quantos, considered one of the greatest kickball players of all time, was asked how he could maintain a 650 percent kicking average he said, 'I kick it where they ain't.'" He paused, looked at Fenton not sure he understood and repeated, "I kick it where…"

"I got it the first time. I'm not stupid." Fenton said angrily and or a moment he wondered if Billy Gilsky sent Chip over to remind him of what happened in yesterday's game to make him feel worse than he already did.

"Indeed you're not Fenton," Chip said as he put his notes in the mailbag and stood to leave. "There are three things Eldon would like you to remember. One, you're not stupid. Two, kick it where they ain't. And three, push here for on," he touched Fenton's right lens, "and here for off," he touched the left one. He grabbed the strap of the mailbag, dragged it across the floor, and opened the door to Fenton's room.

"Wait," Fenton panicked. "How does it help? What does it do?"

Chip looked at him fondly and said, "Remember the first point."

While Fenton was trying to figure out what he meant, he heard the mailbag bounce down the steps, the front door close, and realized Chip had gone.

It took him a moment to see it but in a corner of the box the glasses came in, was a circle formed by the words, Wish Wizards Inc. He squinted and saw, in the center of the circle, the wishbone of a turkey.

Fenton sat up when his mother knocked on the door to his room and said breakfast would be ready in five minutes. He'd fallen asleep at his desk and a flash card with a spelling word on it was stuck to his forehead. He removed the card, looked at it and tried to remember if ain't was on the spelling list. When he stood, he thought he had the flu. Things were moving around on his glasses; he could see his father sitting at the kitchen table reading the newspaper and his mother putting cereal in his bowl.

When he pushed his glasses in place, the scene in the kitchen disappeared, and his room returned to normal. "That's odd," Fenton muttered as he opened the door to his closet to pick out what he would wear to school.

On the bus Billy Gilsky slid into the seat next to him. "I know you don't like surprises, so I'm telling you now so you'll have time to think about it. Okay?"

Fenton shrugged and said, "Okay."

"I just found out, after lunch the safety patrol is going to the gym for crosswalk training."

Fenton waited. If that was the surprise he didn't get what Billy was telling him. You have to be in fourth grade to be on the safety patrol

"Those not going to the gym will be in Ms Chalmer's room." It was obvious to Billy, Fenton didn't understand what he was talking about so he got to the point. "We're playing the fourth grade in kickball during afternoon recess."

Fenton's shoulders sagged. If a team was selected from his class to play the fourth grade, he wouldn't be on it and he'd spend today's recess sitting in the bleachers, watching other kids play the game he loved. He felt so bad he almost missed it when Billy said, "We're kind of low on players so you're starting in right field."

"Really?" That changed everything. He'd have a chance to make up for his mistake in yesterday's game. He'd show them he was as good a kickball player as the next kid unless the next kid was Misty Eindorf who's the best kickball player in school.

They'd played three innings and nothing had been kicked to right field, there seldom was. This time it wasn't just right field, nothing had made it out of the infield. There was one foul ball that Jimmy Debow caught before colliding with the first baseman.

The players knew the school bell would ring any minute, calling them back to class, and ending the game in a scoreless tie. The third grade was up and Billy Gilsky kicked a long fly to left field that was caught. Bobby Fisher tried to bunt his way on base but was thrown out before he reached first.

Fenton was up. As he walked to the plate, he saw Chip sitting in the bleachers. He waved his arms to get Fenton's attention and when he was sure he was watching, touched a finger to the right lens of his glasses.

Fenton remembered his visit and there being something different about his glasses. Had he dreamed it? he wondered, or read about it somewhere?

"Step on it Tug, we don't have all day," the third baseman yelled and brought Fenton back to the task at hand.

He went through his normal pre-kick routine. He tapped the heel of his right foot on home plate, touched the cuff of his pant leg with his left hand, took a deep breath, and lifted his shoulders a few times, trying to relax. The last thing he did before stepping to the plate and hollering, "Slow and smooth," was push his glasses in place. He missed the frame and touched the right lens.

Suddenly he saw clouds of swirling snow that eventually came together to form the words, *Colossal Computers Presents, Playground Wizard 2nd Edition.*

"Strike one," the catcher shouted as he tossed the ball back to the pitcher.

There was more snow and the words, *"Amaze your teammates and baffle your opponents,"* slowly moved across the lens of his glasses.

"Strike two," the catcher yelled.

The last thing Fenton saw was, *"Kick it where they ain't."* Then things cleared and looked they way they usually did.

Just before the pitcher rolled the ball, the outfielders ran toward the infield and the first and second baseman executed the Tug Shift and slid toward second base.

The crowd in the stands yelled,

> **"Fenton can't count.**
> **And he can't see.**
> **He missed two pitches**
> **and he's going to make it three."**

As the ball rolled toward him, Fenton looked where the right fielder had been and thought if it's good enough for Quantos, it's good enough for me. He kicked the ball perfectly and watched it sail over Danny Croup's outstretched hands as he was running at full speed toward the infield.

The ball landed where the fielder had been, rolled across the foul line, and came to rest against a postman's mailbag. Fenton circled the bases and when he jumped on home plate, he was surrounded by his teammates who cheered and lifted him to their shoulders.

The bell rang and on the way back to class all Billy Gilsky could talk about was Fenton's kick and how this was the first time in the history of Buffalo Bill Cody Elementary the third grade had beaten the fourth in anything.

As he walked up the path, Fenton glanced back and saw the ball was there but the mailbag was gone.

That's okay, he thought as he pushed his glasses in place, I'll take it from here.

Would you like to see your manuscript become a book?

If you are interested in becoming a PublishAmerica author, please submit your manuscript for possible publication to us at:

acquisitions@publishamerica.com

You may also mail in your manuscript to:

**PublishAmerica
PO Box 151
Frederick, MD 21705**

We also offer free graphics for Children's Picture Books!

www.publishamerica.com

PublishAmerica

CPSIA information can be obtained at www.ICGtesting.com
Printed in the USA
LVOW050409090113

314917LV00001B/58/P